I'm By Myself, But Still Not Alone

By Shirley A. Johnson

ISBN: 978-1-7361227-0-9

Copyright - 1-9728985281

Table of Contents

Dedication

I dedicate this book to the first childhood friend I can remember, Earlene Smith, and to some of the best adult friends any person can ever have: Vivian McKinney, who was there for me through a long illness and divorce; Elsie Louise Ricks, who has stood by me through triumphs on the mountaintop and tragedies in the valley; and Elease Frederick, Ph.D., who has been the voice of reason in my life for many, many years.

Lastly, I dedicate this book to my sister, Ada, who is the glue that has kept our family connected as a unit since the death of our parents. Thank you all for being there, even when my life's screen was turned off.

Preface

I hope the reader will draw strength from situations in these pages about life as seen through the main character, Beverly Martin--where she has been and where God brought her from. I also hope that the reader will realize that God never fails us; all we must do is believe and wait on Him. I also hope that the reader will understand that you should not be bitter about things in your past, just get better at living in the now because there is a big difference between bitter and better, and the difference is the letter "I." I had to make the choice; each of us gets to make the choice.

Chapter 1: That Lingering Feeling

From my childhood in Coltonville, Georgia, I can only remember bits and pieces of things in my life. My name is Beverly Martin: I am now 2 years old. I remember one afternoon in the summer of 1952, my mommy and daddy left us at home alone and I had a very scary and traumatic experience. Back in the early '50s most Blacks did not live in homes like there are today with modern conveniences and all the necessities, for that matter. Our house was no exception. No locks on the doors or windows, just a wooden latch; no alarms or locks and screens over the windows, and they were very easy to climb through. I was probably about 2 years old, as I said. My older sisters and I were on the front porch. I do remember that day as vividly as if it were yesterday.

Borden County in Georgia was a rural, pastoral farming area. Our house was situated near a wooded area in close proximity to a railroad track. Neighbors were few and far between. There were no rolling hills or picturesque mountains, just flat green land, tall trees, and blue sky as far as the eyes could see. That was the makeup of the land in the area. My dad loved that land and he put in many hours working it, tilling the soil and growing crops. That is how he made a living for our family.

During that time, the train passing on the nearby railroad tracks was the highlight of most summer days, unless we got to go to town with my daddy to sell some produce or pick up supplies from the general store. Hobos were common sights along the railroad tracks, especially in the summertime. We were always told that hobos were harmless, and they walked along the tracks so they could hitch a ride on the trains from one place to another. I did not know what that meant at the time, but later surmised that they had no particular place to be and they would just catch a ride on the train to wherever it was going and they would be satisfied with that.

On this particular day when a hobo appeared, it was quite different than usual. Just as fate would have it, there, as bright as daylight, appeared a haggard old man with a hobo sack hanging over his shoulder. We had seen many of them, but they never came up to our house. He appeared out of the woods just across from it. He turned and looked in our direction and it almost seems as if I could read his mind that said, "Good pickings for this nice bright day." Of course, I know he was not even saying that...probably just wanted a sip of water. Anyway, my sisters, who incidentally were much older than me, were not taking any chances. They whisked me up and we ran into the house.

I was so very much afraid and at that time I thought if I breathed, he would hear me and come in and get me. Well, I heard one of my sisters say as she slammed the door shut and latched it,

"He's coming straight for the porch." Even then, I felt something inside calming me and I could feel warmth around me as if someone was hugging me. At 2 years old, I could sense that presence of something even though at that age I had no idea what it was. After what seemed like many hours, which was probably about two or three minutes, he went away. However, we did not venture back outside. We stayed inside huddled together on the floor beneath the window. You would think that we would hide someplace else since the window was so easy to get into, but we didn't. We just huddled there safe, and no harm came to us.

Later when our parents returned, we told the story step by step, and you know I was trying to tell them how scared I was, but everybody's voice seemed to overpower what I had to say. I think it was around that time that I invented my imaginary friend, who would later evolve into an entire family. Anyway, that is not the last that you will hear about my imaginary Bobette and her family, nor have you heard for the last time about that strange feeling that surrounded me which I started calling my invisible "Comforter" that I have always felt had a presence near me at all times.

A few years passed, and my daddy had another house built that was bigger and nicer. This new house seemed like it was far away from the railroad tracks, when in fact it was just a few miles up the road. We had more neighbors, but that did not bother me because I had my friend Bobette and my Comforter. There were three or four houses in a row at the end of a long path with rows of tall trees on both sides. I could not have been too much older because I vaguely remember that I was not yet in school. I can also tell that I was still very young because I could not understand why someone got a whipping, especially when they had done nothing to deserve it. Mind you, now, I had never gotten one (a whipping) before because I don't remember doing anything to get one. But it was at this time that I did get one. Until this day, I do not know what I did wrong. All I know is that my daddy sent for the switches and I tried to hide under a wood-frame chair, which had no cover to hide me. Of course, all he had to do was pick up the chair and reach down and pick me up. He did whip me along with my sister, but it did not hurt because I had my Comforter to protect me.

Long after the memory of the actual contact of the switch with my skin was gone, I wondered in silence, "What did I do wrong?" Although I was talking to myself, something strange outside of my head whispered softly, "Don't worry about it, all is forgiven, just look ahead." Many days and nights passed as I wandered around the house, around the yard. By myself or in a crowd, I never seemed to be alone and there was an inner peace that always let me know that everything was alright. At a pre-school age I had no idea what this strange feeling was. My parents talked about God and I heard about God and Heaven at church and so forth, but I didn't understand at that time what it had to do with me. Little did I know that the Comforter of which I always felt the presence of was simply God watching over me.

GOLDEN NUGGETS FOR GROWTH #1

Parents should make a point of explaining to their children what they did wrong before punishing them. Whatever method the punishment is, afterward the parents should tell them again why they needed to be punished and make sure the children understand what they should have done instead. Parents need to be attentive to some of the consequences that criticism and disciplining children using punitive methods can have on them. Some of them have harsh results that have long-term ill effects on children, their actions, and overall feelings about the parent-child relationship, even though the discipline doesn't seem very harsh at the time it is administered. Let your children know that you chastised them because you love them. If you don't, those time outs and "constructive" criticisms can be harmful if the child does not understand the reason for them.

WHAT SCRIPTURE SAYS ABOUT INSTRUCTION FOR CHILDREN:

Deuteronomy 6:7 (KJV)--"And thou shall teach them diligently unto thy children..."

Care and diligence are to be used, and pains taken, to instruct children, as soon as they are capable, in the knowledge of God, and of His Commandments.

Hebrews 12:11 (KJV)--"Now no chastening for the present seemeth to be joyous, but grievous: nevertheless, afterward it yieldeth the peaceable fruit of righteousness unto them which are exercised thereby."

For the moment, all discipline seems painful rather than pleasant, but later it yields the peaceful fruit of righteousness to those who have been trained by it.

Chapter 2: The Early Years

As the years passed, I remembered only more bits and pieces. I do remember that I was a happy child, with my imaginary family, but I preferred to be alone most of the time. I remember that my sister who was closest to me in age was not nice to me. In fact, she was downright unkind and callous. We shared the same bed growing up, and she would come to bed with open pins and use them if I touched any part of her body. My feet probably had as many holes as a pin cushion during those days because she was always sticking those pins in them when my feet would even get close to her in bed. Never mind all of that, I would say my prayers like a good little girl and go on to bed, and even though the pins did hurt, I would soon forget about them. After all, she was my sister! And I would go on to sleep.

I had a propensity for itching when I thought something was dirty or stained, especially if the weather was cold (in fact even now, as an adult, I feel that way). When my parents would take me someplace that seemed dirty to me, or had soiled cushions or carpets, etc., I would become very uncomfortable and my skin would itch and itch. The only thing that seemed to help was to go home and bury myself in the bed under those heavy quilts that my mommy used to make by hand. That seemed to make me safe, and I felt that my Comforter was there soothing me. I now realize there is a term for what I had, called a phobia. Yes, I had a phobia about unclean things and places.

I remember one day, a teenager from the neighborhood whom I'll call Bernard came over to visit with my sisters while my parents were gone. As you remember, they were much older than me. There had been a rumor that Bernard had lice, which, of course, was not true. You know how insensitive some teenagers can be. Today, spreading rumors like that would be considered a form of bullying. Well, they wouldn't let him sit down, but did not ask him to leave. I, of course, did not know that it was just a rumor, and I started itching so much I ran to my mommy's bed and buried myself under her quilts and not only prayed to stop itching, I also prayed for Bernard to be rid of the lice. I thought he had a disease or something, yet I had compassion for him. I had love and compassion for people because I felt like someone whom I could not see had love and compassion for me. Even then, as a little girl, I was just as interested in the well-being of others as I was for myself. I found out later the rumor surfaced in the neighborhood because nobody wanted Bernard as their "so-called" boyfriend. That itching phobia carried right over into my adulthood, but now I believe it to be just a nervous condition.

As time passed, I continued to cling to my imaginary friend and her family. I went to school, I interacted with other people, and yet I felt that I was different. I loved being at home, usually some place by myself. No matter what my parents bought me in the way of clothes, I always kept one outfit for that special occasion (I didn't really know what); I envisioned some special occasion. I kept that special outfit hanging in the wardrobe and would not wear it, even on Sundays when we got all dressed up in our "good clothes" and patent leather shoes. My mommy never made me wear it, when I didn't volunteer to take it out.

My family was big; you can almost say that I had a three-part family. I had my older sisters and also siblings who were much younger than I was. Elementary school was hard for me because I was always a loner, even though others wanted to be my friend. School was also hard because we had to walk when it was hot; when it was not so hot, we still had to walk. There was a white-board-framed, three-room school approximately three miles from our house. I attended that school the first two years of my schooling. I now know that it was called a Rosenwald School, which I'll explain later. I don't remember a lot of things that happened during those two years. I do remember that at the front of each of the three rooms, there was a long narrow room with hooks. We called that the coat room, a place where I never wanted to leave my coat and hat.

We need always to show compassion for others; show kindness, caring, and a willingness to help others. Compassion is a word for a very positive emotion that has to do with being thoughtful and decent. Compassion gives us the ability to understand someone else's situation and the desire to take action to improve their lives. For people who are dependent on others for help and support, compassion is often the most important factor. Compassion is strength. It is much easier to slap someone you think is an enemy than to offer a hand up. True strength is gentle and fair and, therefore, showing mercy is a sign of strength. Compassion allows one to understand others and see that they are more like us than different. The Bible tells about a God who has compassion for Israel. It tells of a Savior who suffers for the world, and it asks us to live and act as Jesus did.

What teenagers in the neighborhood did to Bernard was cruel and ungodly. It all started because nobody wanted to be around him; nobody wanted him to identify with them. I suspect those same teenagers saw something in Bernard that reminded them of something they did not like about themselves. Compassion for him would have been a step up in fixing the traits they disliked in themselves.

WHAT SCRIPTURE SAYS ABOUT COMPASSION:

Isaiah 63:7 (NIV)--"I will tell of the kindness of the Lord, the deeds for which he is to be praised, according to all the Lord has done for us — yes, the many good things he has done for Israel, according to his compassion and many kindness."

Ephesians 4:32--"Be kind and compassionate to one another, forgiving each other, just as Christ God forgave you."

Chapter 3: Estheree, Friend for Life

Aside from my imaginary family, I chose one little girl to be my best friend when I was in third grade. Her name was Estheree and she was special, that is why I chose her as a friend.

For the longest time, I had had my imaginary family to comfort me and keep me company. However, I now had a real person not only for comfort but companionship. This person was someone I could talk to about my imaginary family out loud, and she would not think I was a lunatic. You see, people, even little girls, don't go around raving about people nobody can see. Estheree was different. She was a real live little girl with whom I had no problems identifying. In my eyes, she was the perfect friend.

I remember the first day of school, in the brand new, nice brick school in town. It was the first day of my third-grade year. The years before third grade, I attended that Rosenwald School I talked about located smack dab in the middle of the rural farming area. As I remember, there was no comparison between this new school and that white-board, three-room school with no heat or running water. Coal was hauled in by the county and piled out back, and the boys used the coal bucket to bring it in to keep the school warm on these winter days.

Rosenwald Schools were financed through a partnership between Julius Rosenwald, a rich northerner, and communities in the South. The purpose for building the schools throughout the South was to provide an education for Black children in the rural South. The first one was built in 1915. By the late 1950s, it was time for more and better schools. The Rosenwald idea was just not enough.

That first day of school, in the new building, was an exciting day. This school had INDOOR PLUMBING! Not many Blacks living in the rural areas were accustomed to having indoor plumbing or the modern conveniences that the new elementary school had to offer. It was also an exciting day because most of the children did not have to walk to the new school, being that it was in town; the school bus was more than a luxury.

As we quickly emerged from the bus and headed for the huge multi-purpose room, which doubled as the school cafeteria, the children moved in a neat single-file line and found themselves corralled in that large room with folding chairs and nice shiny tables. The aroma of food was already gravitating from the kitchen located behind the multi-purpose room/cafeteria when we filed in and took our seats. We waited patiently as our names were called to line up behind different teachers who were standing like soldiers, dressed more like they were getting ready for Sunday church service than going to a classroom.

I was chosen, along with about 26 other boys and girls, for the third grade "A" class. I thought to myself, "A" must mean that we are the smartest. I don't know why, but it seemed that Estheree and I naturally gravitated to each other. When we got to the classroom, the teacher said that we could sit wherever we liked. I said to myself, "We must be the smart bunch, because we get to choose." Estheree and I found desks, naturally at the front of the class, near the window. At the window, I could watch what was happening outside around the outskirts of town as well as stay honed in on what was going on in the classroom. I knew she would be a best friend for keeps. I guess I liked her so much because I could see a lot of myself in her. Even from the beginning of our friendship, we could almost finish one another's sentences. The day was pleasant, and I almost forgot about my imaginary family until Estheree and I went our separate ways at the end of the day to find the bus that would be traveling our routes home.

When I got home that afternoon, I didn't tell much about what happened that day at school, although I was quizzed by everybody until I went to bed that night. The next morning, I looked forward to a new adventure at school. Before leaving, I quickly made plans for what my "make-believe" family would do today. Then I was off to wait for my bus to come.

It just so happened that our buses arrived at school precisely at the same time. Both Estheree and I carried a lunch pail swinging back and forth as we entered the school building that morning and most every other morning. You see, although we had a shiny new school with a Spic and Span cafeteria, we seldom went through the lunch line. My mommy always packed my lunch and it was only when she had not had a chance to make a fresh loaf of bread the day before that I got to go through the lunch line. It really did not matter to me because I enjoyed eating those thick slices of yeast bread that my mommy had cut precisely the same size from the giant loaves of bread she baked in our big polished wood-burning oven.

Each day at lunch, Estheree and I would sit at the end of the long row of tables in the cafeteria, open our lunch boxes, carefully unwrap our sandwiches and take a bite, take a sip of milk from the square-shaped, waxed container that we bought for 3 cents, and carry on a conversation all to ourselves. It seemed that we could get lost for that 30-minute period, and everybody around us became invisible. Although we sat together at the end of that long table each day, I never ever looked to see or bothered to ask if the bread for her sandwich was store-bought or homemade. I guess that was not something high on my list of priorities to know. In other words, it probably would not have mattered.

At recess time, we always had something creative to play and all the other children crowded around out of curiosity to see what we were doing. Unless the teacher said that we had to participate in a group game, we would simply move away from them to another spot and they would lose interest and go about their way. We could even develop a way to come down the playground slide that was creative.

I told Estheree about my imaginary family and she got to know them very well. Sometimes, I would even invite her to join me in a visit with them (in our minds, of course). She would just laugh and I remember vividly, she would fall back on her hands and her thick braids would swing in the air. In the classroom we were competitive, but still quickly came to each other's aid, if we were having problems figuring out how to find an answer. The teacher called us the "Bobbsey Twins," after the main characters of the popular children's books. She sometimes treated us special because we were smart and never caused any trouble.

As long as we had been friends, I had never seen Estheree cry. This one day was an exception. It was in the early fall and our school was getting ready for the huge "chapel program." Today we call them assembly programs or pageants. All the grade levels were assembled in that shiny new cafeteria that doubled as the multi-purpose room when we had programs. Altogether, there were about seven classes and as many teachers in the place. Each teacher was gathering students for specific acting parts. Mrs. Pettigrew was grouping students together as part of the singing forest animal group. She had chosen several students, Estheree included, before she walked over to me and said, "Stand up." I did, and she said, you should do just fine with this group. After she had completed her choices for her clan, she told us that unlike the other students in the stage performance, we would have to stay after school each day for practice because our parts were much more difficult than others.

I know my mommy did not drive and my father would not be able to stop work and come to pick me up each afternoon. (Be mindful now, this was the mid '50s and things were not as they are today); neighbors and friends didn't have a second car. Some of them didn't even have one car. I slowly raised my hand to point that out. She did not see my hand, so I called her name. I guess she didn't like me interrupting her, because she turned around with fire in her eyes. My thought was, "Who are you and what have you done with Mrs. Pettigrew?" She yelled so loudly that I could feel the floor move, "What do you want?" Everybody stopped and the room became silent. I had never been at a loss for words, but at that moment, my words seemed to be frozen in my mouth. After what seemed like forever, I finally said, "I can't stay after school because I have nobody to pick me up." She grabbed me by my arm and shoved me so hard I almost fell to the floor. "Get over there and sit down then," she snorted, "And stop wasting my time. Why didn't you say so in the first place?"

I felt about two inches tall and I could feel a warm tear well up in my eye and fall to my cheek. Nobody came to my rescue and nobody said a word, except Estheree. She came to my side with tears streaming down her face. She whispered to me, "It's alright, nobody wants to be in that old stupid play anyway." I still can't really remember what happened after that. But I could feel a silent calm come over me and it felt as if something or someone was cradling me. I had had that feeling before and would have it come over me many, many times after that...the same feeling that I had the day the hobo came too close to my house, when I was just a toddler. For a long time, I could not understand why Mrs. Pettigrew treated me that way or why none of the other teachers said or did nothing. But I did realize one thing: Estheree was precious and would be a friend for life.

I did not get a part in the pageant and Estheree didn't perform either. When we returned to the classroom, she told our teacher she did not want to participate. The only thing the teacher said was, "I understand." I never told my parents what happened at school that day. To me it did not matter anymore and was not worth retelling.

After that episode, Mrs. Pettigrew continued as though nothing had happened. Every time I saw her, I could picture the fire in her eyes that day in the multi-purpose room. Something inside me made me forgive her, but I still prayed each night for the remainder of the year that I would never, ever be in her class.

For the remainder of my stay in elementary school, I always hoped and prayer that Mrs. Pettigrew would not be my teacher. I really did not think there were enough imaginary families or Comforters in the world to help me deal with her. I did, however, get a gem of a teacher in fifth grade. Her name was Mrs. Ollie Mae Flagstaff, and a flag staff she was. She was the best teacher anyone could ever have, and she was kind to everybody. Besides, she knew my parents and my uncle, who worked at the local wholesale market (another name for a meat market). He even brought her to school each day. She didn't drive. She also had a sister who rode with them and taught fourth grade down the hall.

Mrs. Flagstaff was a straight-up bonafide Christian. She put God in everything she taught, from reading to arithmetic, I mean it, from A to Z. Devotion each morning was like a church service. We were allowed to pray and say Bible verses back then. That was before "the world" got into everybody's business. I really don't think what she did in her classroom was what the school board had in mind when they thought about morning devotion. She taught us more Bible verses than the Sunday School teacher did. She applied things in everyday like to Scripture and pointed it out in practical ways. We could recite entire chapters of the Bible by the time we left fifth grade. In her classroom, more so than at church, is where I really learned about that feeling that often came over me...the Comforter. Mrs. Flagstaff taught the lessons, she taught the Bible, she loved the children, she told us why we should forgive people, and she provided for everybody. Fifth grade was the best I could ask for--a nice, firm but fair teacher and the most precious friend anyone could ask for, Estheree.

Just before school closed for the summer, it was Mrs. Flagstaff's turn to have her class present an assembly program. You know she had planned to have every character in the Bible in our program (just kidding), but it was close to it. The night before the assembly program, I went in the wardrobe in my bedroom and picked out my sky blue dress that I had been saving for a special time, I didn't think there would be a time more special than this, because I loved Mrs. Flagstaff and wanted very much to please her. My mommy did not give me plaits that day; she made me two puffy ponytails and a big fluffy bang in front. I waited and waited for the bus, but it never came. My mommy couldn't take me to school because she could not drive. All she could do was sit on the step and wait for the bus with me. Two hours went by and the bus came. When our bus got to school, the assembly was almost over. Other students in the class had taken the parts that we who were on the late bus had practiced. I was heartbroken; however, I felt better when I learned that Estheree had taken my part and had done a good job, too. Mrs. Flagstaff, trying to make me feel better said, "You might not have been here for the play, but you are one of the prettiest students in the building today."

I had thought about it before, but after that day, I often wondered where Mrs. Flagstaff was the day Mrs. Pettigrew lashed into me back in third grade. I doubt if Mrs. Pettigrew remembered or ever thought of that incident ever again. When I would see her around the school, I would sometimes think of going to her, telling her that I forgave her for what she did to me, but as quickly as the notion came into my head, it disappeared. But I did forgive her. She died when I was a young adult. I had put all of that behind me, but I never have forgotten it. Now as an adult and a seasoned Christian, I understand how and why I forgave her.

GOLDEN NUGGETS FOR GROWTH #3

When our burdens become too heavy for us to carry, God sometimes puts someone in our path to help us get through those valley experiences. At other times he simply carries our burden, our cross, AND us. When all is said and done, the Holy Spirit helps us forgive.

Please be mindful that children remember most of the things that happen to them as they go through life; oftentimes, they remember the bad things and people who caused them hurt and treated them unjustly more vividly then they remember the good things. Even though they forgive, they rarely forget.

Forgiveness is not minimizing the offense or the hurt. Forgiveness is not forgetting what happened. You can remember the past, but you don't have to relive the pain. Forgiving someone does not mean you have to go on vacation with them. What someone did to you is not OK or fair, but forgiveness is not about fairness. Forgiveness is having faith that God will take care of it...that God is the judge–and you don't have to be.

WHAT SCRIPTURE SAYS ABOUT FORGIVENESS:

Ephesians 4:31-32 (NLT)--"Get rid of all bitterness, rage, anger, harsh words, and slander, as well as all types of evil behavior. Instead, be kind to each other, tenderhearted, forgiving one another, just as God through Christ has forgiven you."

Romans 12:19 (NLT)--"Dear friends, never take revenge. Leave that to the righteous anger of God. For the Scriptures say, 'I will take revenge; I will pay them back,' says the LORD."

Lamentations 3:58-59 (NIV)--"O Lord, you took up my case; you redeemed my life. You have seen, O LORD, the wrong done to me. Uphold my cause!"

Chapter 4: My Imaginary Family

Now I think it is time to introduce you to my imaginary family. It has been almost 10 years since I created them but, you know, only one of them has a name. There is a father, mother, and several siblings, but the only important one in the family is the one that I created to be most like me. Her name, if you remember, is Bobette. Bobette is my age and she lived with her family in an A-frame-shaped, two-story white stick house with three additional rooms in a line on the back of the first floor. This house is not at all like my real house, but I would like for it to be. I imagined that this house is in a little community near the town where I live. It is always exciting to go there in my imagination because there is always something exciting going on in that household.

The house has two bedrooms upstairs; one of them belongs to Bobette and she gets to do whatever she wants to in that room. She doesn't even have a sister who sticks her with pins when she goes to bed at night. A teenaged sister occupies the room right next to her, across the hall. That's OK with Bobette because her sister is a teenager and is not interested in what's happening across the way and, anyway, her door is always closed. You won't get any complaints from Bobette; the more her door is closed the more privacy for my little friend. The mother and father have a room on the first floor; right side and directly behind their room is another bedroom where the two youngest boys sleep. Across the hall on the first floor is the living room and a bedroom directly behind that. This is the bedroom of the two oldest girls. Behind that bedroom are two rooms making an L shape at the back of the house. Those rooms are the kitchen and the room where the family eats meals, but not necessarily a dining room.

I know there is wondering about why the two oldest girls are sharing a room downstairs. Well, as you remember, this is MY imaginary family and I situate them the way I want my ideal family to be.

As I imagined it, there was always lots of excitement in the house, someone was always coming or going or having a party or taking a road trip, getting something new or something. Although there is excitement, Bobette does not seem to mind. I make it all up in my head and then what Bobette does, I keep separate. Typical of how my life is in my real family...separate.

I made the neighborhood real cool and my imaginary family were pillars of the community; however, I sprinkled a few not-so-respectable characters in. You see, I wanted to create situations that I could rationalize and justify as I tried to understand parts of the things happening in my real life. Sometimes, I would have the parents say when the children went out, "Now stay away from that bad crowd." I heard that statement quite a bit in my real family. At 10 or so years old, I could not really envision why my parents would call someone in the community "bad." So, to try to understand, I made up my own rational reasons and then disclaimed them through the actions of Bobette and her family. I guess I had my reasons for imagining them. It didn't really matter because I was determined to prove, through Bobette, that there is good in everybody.

As I went about my business with my imaginary family, dressing them, having conversations with them, sending them on short errands and long trips, in the back of my mind I would always have an imaginary task for Bobette. One day, I pretended that she was going to the neighborhood playground, which consisted of a dirt ball field and a few swings made of rope tied from tall oak trees, and a couple of slides. Bobette decided (I decided that Bobette) would not stay away from that "bad" crowd. In my mind's eye, I would prove that the ways of some people might be bad, but people themselves are not bad. I pretended that as she approached the park, one of the older men from the neighborhood was sitting on a broken bench near the swings, drinking something from a bottle hidden in a bag. Ignoring what she had been told, I pretended that she stopped to talk to him. Bobette asked, "What's that you're drinking?" The old man replied, "Something you don't need to know about. It makes hair grow on your chest," he said. I don't know what it meant but I had heard someone use the phrase before, and I thought it sounded good for her to say. She asked what that meant. He said, "Well, I guess I might as well start at the beginning."

The old man started to tell her how one day he lost his job and he didn't feel much like going home to his family, so he stopped by the local store and purchased a bottle. He thought he would drown his misery in that bottle. Well, the only thing it did was make him do and say things he had no business saying. That is what he called, "growing hair on his chest." Anyway, I made up a good story to tell. He went back to his former workplace, raised the roof (put up a big fuss), chased the owner down the street, and said a lot of choice words to the onlookers.

To make a long story short, what he did reflected badly on his entire family, not just at his house but at all of his relatives' homes. And, as a matter of fact, it landed him in jail. That made him even more bitter and angry when the whole ordeal was over. It had turned into something he could not fix. Over the years, he drifted away from his family, but the damage was done. He couldn't fix it and they all had been labeled. It was especially hard for him because it affected his young children more than anybody. They just could not understand why the townspeople wanted nothing to do with them. They were suffering all because of him. Every time he started to think about what he did all those years before, he would become sad, so he would go get a bottle and try to drown his sorrow in the bottle. I knew a real person like him who lived in town. My daddy always said, "Ol' Boo Jack won't work in a pie shop." One time when he said it my little brother asked, "Daddy if he won't work in a pie shop, why don't you give him a job helping you on the farm?" Everybody is still laughing about that even today.

I imagined this story because I knew people in my real community who were treated that way and I never knew why. My parents never said; they would just tell us to stay away from them. It never dawned on me to ask why everybody thought they were so different. So, that is why I made up the story with this twist. It was my way of rationalizing what happened, why it happened, and how it could be fixed. My inner self had to find a way to fix it if I could, through Bobette. I felt if I could fix an imaginary problem, I could probably fix a real one. It was at that time that I gave her the inner feeling that I had felt from time to time all my life...inner safety, warmth, and compassion. Through her, I could say to someone, "It's going to be alright."

I spent most of that afternoon with my imaginary Bobette and the old man, figuring out how to help him, how to make things right for him again. The more I imagined, the more I came to realize that the world has a good bit of cold uncaring people who are not concerned about others. Often, people who are not God fearing do not understand the emotions of others, and they have little empathy for other people. They do not get what others are feeling, so it is impossible for them to place themselves in another person's situation. I learned that from Sunday School.

The more I imagined, the more I thought about my own family. I wondered if they really knew why they called some people "bad." Or if they had really tried to understand why those people did what they did. My parents like others in the community were reasonable, compassionate people, so why did they say these things about certain people? Had they ever tried to fix any of those situations? Had they ever tried to reach out to them? I guess for them it was easier to just go with the status quo. Like we often say today, "People don't really want to help those who are lost, they just want to pretend to care." They don't really care that those who are not doing well, will get a chance to do better." Case in point: Whom do we socialize with? Whom do we invite to our church when we are having a special service? The answer is...people who are just like us...people who do the same things we do and think like us.

Well, through Bobette, I had good practice for the real world. Bobette told the old man that what happened to his family was not really his fault. He did make a mistake, but the community put the bull's-eye on his family's backs. Through Bobette, I invited the old man to stop trying to drown himself in whatever was in the bottle, but instead look for the Comforter that she had found who was guaranteed to give him a warm feeling and a safe place within himself to go.

GOLDEN NUGGET FOR GROWTH #4

In everyday life, people find it so easy to pass judgments on others when they do not really know the whole story. We cannot make someone else happy unless we are happy ourselves. Sometimes, we must let our inner self take over and, yes, imagine that by the Grace of God, there goes you. Once that is done, it is easier to understand and sympathize from the point of view of others. Jesus set the greatest example for us to love one another in practical and compassionate ways. If we would just follow his example, we will not see human beings as bad people, but will better see that they just have undesirable traits. If we avoid them and never try to help them, those bad ways may become justified in them and may continue to fester.

WHAT SCRIPTURE SAYS ABOUT EMPATHING WITH AND NOT JUDGING:

James 4:11-12 (ESV)--"Do not speak evil against one another, brothers. The one who speaks against a brother or judges his brother, speaks evil against the law and judges the law. But if you judge the law, you are not a doer of the law but a judge. There is only one lawgiver and judge, he who is able to save and to destroy. But who are you to judge your neighbor?"

James 2:13 (ESV)--"For judgment is without mercy to one who has shown no mercy. Mercy triumphs over judgment."

Matthew 7:11 (ESV)--"Judge not, that ye be not judged."

CHAPTER 5: Growing Older

By the time I reached middle school in 1962, things were different. I no longer relied so much on my imaginary family and Estheree was gone. In middle school we had to go to feeder schools. Because Estheree lived in a different section of the county, we were bused to different middle schools. My new school was 15 miles away in another town. Although it was not that many miles away, it seemed more like 100 miles. Estheree and I almost never saw each other anymore. No phone calls or visits because in the early '60s, few people had telephones, and letter writing to be sent through the mail was not something that a 12-year-old did on a routine basis. Occasionally, one of my older sisters would drive me to Estheree's house for a little while, but they would never leave me, so I did not get to stay long. She lived with her grandparents and they did not have a car. Her uncle, who lived next door, generally took them where they needed to go. However, bringing Estheree to my house was out of the question.

My new school was no different than the one I left, but the climate was different in more ways than one. There seemed to be two different cultures within the one school. About half of the student body lived in town and the other half was bused in from the rural areas nearby.

As a young girl, I was used to living in a rural area and I did not really like associating with a lot of new people. However, by this stage in my life I had acquired a lot of other interests and I had more variety in my life. I had all but abandoned my imaginary family. When I needed a pick-me-up, I could always go back to "the family" and Bobette to just make up my own situations when I wanted to. Bobette was still my true lifeline and she always filled the bill. No, there was nothing like Bobette except, of course, Estheree. I missed her a lot. But I was smart, resourceful, and everybody liked me, so I could manage. I had even started to come around and open up, even when I did not have to.

Back in my old elementary school, my class had formed a relationship with one of the classes at the elementary school that was a part of this middle-school campus. Once each six weeks we would write letters to a pen pal. After doing that for a while, I have become familiar with what the school was like. Some of those pen pal students were actually in my new class. That turned out to be a plus for me. My pen pal's name was Alice. Upon arrival that first day, I got the opportunity to meet her, not through words on a sheet of paper, but in person. She was nothing like what I had pictured her to be and she was nothing like the energetic young girl in the letters I received. We were more like oil and water and she certainly was no Estheree. Alice was pale and sickly looking. At recess time, she just hung around the teacher and, at lunch, she would just sit silently and nibble on her food, throwing most of it away at the end of the lunch period. She was smart enough, but she never wanted to talk...she was not shy, just didn't have the same kind of "with-it-ness" that I had envisioned from reading the letters I received from her every six weeks in elementary school. But at least she and some of the other students were familiar to me from the information I gained through the letters. They considered me to be a friend and I felt like I had known them from the beginning.

I later found out that Alice had a chronic illness, which accounted for her peculiar behavior (she was not sick when we were pen pals back in elementary school). I always went out of my way to be kind to her and she would just smile and stay silent. Early in the spring, Alice went away to the hospital and she never returned to school. Once, our class sent her a great big get-well card. I also included her in my prayers every night. One day her mother came to the school and our teacher took her into the hallway to talk. Later, as our class was going to lunch, I heard my teacher telling the teacher next door that Alice would not be back. Her family was moving to the big city to be near the hospital for her treatments. I never saw or heard from Alice again.

My life was certainly "turning a corner." I was getting more responsibility at home, and at school many of my friends looked at me as the leader (I really do not know where that came from). My middle-school years were proving to be quite an experience. On days when the weather was warm, I liked sitting in the back seat of my father's green Ford Fairlane after school to do my homework. There, I would do my homework, look up at the clouds, and imagine that I was on an airplane taking a trip. This would be a pleasant time until my younger sisters and brother discovered my hiding place and wanted to join me. Although that back seat could hold four people, in my opinion it was not enough space for me and them, too. Besides, that was considered my alone time. I soon abandoned that space in the back seat of the Ford Fairlane for a more comfortable space on the thick throw rug behind the couch in the living room. That was an ideal place because nobody ever went in the living room unless it was Sunday and we had company. Sometimes my parents gave the OK for a fella, if they liked him, to come over and talk with my older sisters who were still at home, but that was usually at night and my daddy would be setting right there in the room with them to make sure they left by 9 o'clock. It was all so funny until later when I got to be their age.

We always watched television in my parents' bedroom because, unlike today, with one in every room, we only owned the one. Even that one was turned off by 9 each night. On the weekends we watched more. My mommy's favorite show on Saturday at noon was Sky King. All of us got a kick out of watching that together as Penny and her Uncle Sky went off in his Cessna airplane to catch the crooks. Sometimes on Saturday evenings, we would go visit my grandmother and eat supper with her. After we ate, we would always watch television, in her bedroom, too. Gunsmoke was my daddy's favorite, and after we watched that we would say our goodbyes and go home. I would often think to myself, what is the point of watching television if you couldn't watch what you wanted to watch?

During these times, we always had a cousin or two who came to live with us, but mostly not at the same time. They were not boys but young men, Joe and Willie. They helped my daddy on the farm. Joe was older and he stayed for a little while then went on to find work elsewhere. Willie was his young brother, but still older than my big sisters. I do not remember exactly why they were living with us because their parents lived not that far away, just in another county. Jobs were not plentiful, so I guess it was kind of a job for them. One time even, one of my cousins, Dorthea, came to live with us, but not to help work on the farm. She liked being with my older sisters and since all her siblings were grown and living in northern cities, her parents let her come and my mommy and daddy did not mind. Her father was my uncle whom I told you about earlier, who worked at the wholesale store and drove Mrs. Flagstaff to school.

One summer when my cousin Willie was living with us, Dorthea also came. My father had what he thought was an economical idea. So, we could have some spending money, he decided to plant an acre of cucumbers with the plan for us to pick them. Willie would supervise, Daddy would take them to the market, and we all would have our own money to spend when we went to town. In order to get the best value, you must pick cucumbers at least every other day so they do not grow too large. Willie showed us how to pick and which ones to look for, explaining that the larger ones were of lesser value. In fact, the largest ones were only good for feeding to the hogs. The more he coached us, the fewer cucumbers we picked. It would be so hot, and these vines would be so itchy, I dreaded even thinking about them. The second day of picking, I filled my bucket with the largest ones I could find and left the field. Although the others did not pick the largest ones, they didn't do much better than me. They found a shade tree to sit under and talk about boys. Dorthea complained that she did not come to get hot and sweaty, she came to have fun and she didn't care if she didn't have any money of her own to spend. That, along with the hot sun, made for the end of our picking. Willie was left all alone in the hot sun picking. My bucket full of huge "cukes" yielded less than a dollar, because most of them had to be fed to the hogs.

What my father could have done was make us come back and finish the job. I guess he was getting soft in his later years because he did not do that. Instead, he went down the road and got some young guys to pick the cucumbers; he took them to market, paid them what they were owed and put the profit in his pocket. When we wanted spending money, he would say, "All of your earnings went to the pickers." We thought he was being unfair, and we told him so. We understood that he had to pay the workers, but we deserved the leftover profits; after all, they were our cucumbers. Willie would sit on the porch at night and laugh until tears ran down his face because he said we got what we deserved. We frustrated him when he was trying to make us work but he, like my daddy, got the last laugh.

By the time I was in seventh grade, I had become quite popular, but I still had my peculiar ways and there were still times when I preferred to be by myself. I think I had long since abandoned the imaginary family, but they were stuck in the back of my imagination, just in case. I was well liked by my peers as well as the adults and I had many friends in school and outside of school. However, none of my friends could compare to Estheree. Although I never saw her much, I still thought about her from time to time and often wondered if I would ever have another friend as close as she was.

In addition to having lots of friends, I had developed the idea that I needed to protect those who needed protecting, just as my Comforter gave me a warm, safe feeling. I wanted to give others that same feeling. One day, we were in science class. The teacher, Ms. Carson, was explaining about weather patterns. You just had to know Ms. Carson, to understand how difficult she could be. She had never been married and, according to some, that accounted for the way she acted. They would say she did not have anything to occupy her time, so she made everybody's life miserable because she was miserable. In her mind, the world would stop turning if things were not prim and in their places.

"Conditions have to match," she said, "for some weather patterns to form." As soon as she finished that sentence, she firmly said to one of the girls in the room, "Come here, Ellen." Ellen got up and walked to the front of the class, puzzled as most of us were. When Ellen was standing beside her, Ms. Carson instructed her to turn around and face the class. What she said next horrified me and all I could think about was that day in third grade when Mrs. Pettigrew yelled at me for no good reason. Ms. Carson asked the class, "If these clothes were weather patterns, do you think they would form? What were you thinking when you got dressed this morning?" she snapped at Ellen. Nobody said a word. She was referring to the plaid skirt and floral blouse Ellen was wearing. Today, those different patterns would be fashionable, but back then they did not match. Ellen bowed her head to hide the tears as they slowly rolled down her face. I could sense the hurt in her heart. I heard a little voice in my head saying, "Beverly, you must do something, must say something!" I swing out of my seat and yelled, "You have no right to criticize anybody's clothes and you don't have the right to say whatever you want to just because you are the teacher." Almost as soon as I had spoken, I realized what I had done, but I thought to myself, "I will face the consequences later, but right now I have to try and fix the horrible wrong this lady has done."

The entire class was sitting there with their eyes bulging and their mouths open in disbelief. By this time, Ellen was openly sobbing, and I walked over and took her by the hand and said, "It's OK, it's OK." I could hear Ms. Carson's voice over mine, saying, "Young lady, you are in big trouble. You are going to the office right now." A voice in the back of the room said, "That won't be necessary. I cannot believe what I just witnessed. Ms. Carson, as soon as I send someone to cover your class, please meet me in my office." When I turned around and looked up, the principal was walking up the aisle between two rows of desks toward the front of the room. He looked at Ellen and asked if she needed to go to the bathroom to get herself together. "Take as much time as you need," he said.

I slumped into my desk and put my head in my hands, thinking, "I am in big trouble now, if not with Ms. Carson, certainly with the principal and then my mommy and daddy." At that point though, I did not care. I felt a warm feeling come over me and wrapped around my entire body as if something were saying, "Well done."

I do not know what happened when Ms. Carson went to the office, because after that, she was still her old grumpy, mean self when she returned. When the bell sounded, and we were dismissed to the next class, as I walked out the door I could almost feel her eyes gazing at my back as I left the room. I do know one thing: She never embarrassed anybody in class again. When I got home, I know my first order of business should be to tell my mommy everything. She would in turn tell my daddy when he got home, and then justice would be served on me. Things did not turn out as I had expected. That evening the only thing my daddy said was, "We are supposed to help those who need help." He also told me that we should not be disrespectful to our elders, but sometimes, when they are wrong, their mistakes are worth pointing out. He said that he was going to wait to see what the principal had to say about this and then he would share his thoughts with the principal. Then he told me to finish my homework and go to bed.

When I went to school the next day, Ellen met me in the hall and thanked me for "sticking up" for her. I replied, "No problem, I know you would have done the same for me." At that moment, I knew I had a new friend for life, not like Estheree, but nevertheless a new friend anyway. I never heard anything else about the subject from the principal, Ms. Carson, or my daddy. I did learn something from that experience, though. Some people in this world do not even know that kindness is an option.

A similar situation occurred one day in my neighborhood. Down the tree-lined road from my house was another family, a mother and her six children. The mother was the housekeeper for a White family in the neighborhood. She was seldom at home during the day and her children mostly cared for themselves. One day after school, one of the girls a year or two older than me walked down the path to my house. We talked sometime on the school bus, but we did not visit much when we were at home although her younger brother often played with my brother. She was looking for her brother and I told her he was on the front porch with my little brother playing with his soldiers. We sat on the trunk of my father's Ford Fairlane and started a conversation about school. The bully of the neighborhood came up the path, walked right into our yard, and pushed her off the car onto the ground. As she started to get up, he said, "You know, I was coming over, so why weren't you at home? For as long as you are my girl, you will obey me." As she was getting up, he raised his hand to hit her. I grabbed a stick and told him if he hit her, I was going to knock him out. I could feel something inside of me saying, "You must do something." Well, both of us were saved by my father. Just at that time my daddy drove up on the tractor. He took care of that bully in short order. He then took her in the Fairlane up to where her mother was working. He let me ride along. He not only told the mother what had happened, but he gave her an ear full of advice. Among the advice was that her daughter was too young to have boys hanging around the house when there were no adults present and that bullies should not be allowed around her children.

I once again felt that it was my calling to come to the rescue. However, in this case it was not necessary because my daddy was there, and I guarantee that bully will think twice before he comes in our yard again or go to the neighbor's house ever again. The mother had no idea her daughter was even seeing him, and she took care of the matter. After that incident was over, the girl told me that she was glad I helped her because she was afraid of him and she was embarrassed that I had to witness that. However, she said that she was more terrified of her mother finding out that she had been seeing him. Although she was older, we became friends. I would sometimes sit beside her on the bus, we would talk sometimes at school, and we did things in the neighborhood sometimes.

As my junior high school years progressed, life was good. My personality started to blossom into somewhat of a leader, and my classmates started to look to me for ideas and strategies. I rather enjoyed the interactions with everybody at school, at home, and everywhere. This was such a different twist from whom I used to be, other than in my imaginary family. One thing did not change: When the chips were down or when things went well and when they did not go so well, I could always sense the presence of my Comforter.

GOLDEN NUGGETS FOR GROWTH #5

When things go in the wrong direction, one's reaction or action may not be the norm, but there comes a time when you need to stand for what you know is right based on what moral humanity dictates and what the Word says. This is true because there is only one certainty in our lives, and for as long as He (God) is there, we can cope with everything else. We must learn how to function on more than one track, for as long as that track is the right track.

Too often, man looks at appearance; as Ms. Carson did with Ellen. Not only did she look at appearance, she also judged her by the standing she thought the student held in society. That was wrong. It never occurred to her to think what Ellen had in her heart...clothes do not make a person; who a person's family members are does not matter; and how popular a person is should not be the bottom line. By Ms. Carson's action, one can tell what is in her heart. She never stopped to measure Ellen's character and inner goodness. She never stopped to have or demonstrate compassion for her fellow man. God sent us into the world to be made beautiful beings, with a holy character, a sweet disposition, an angelic life. Let us live for our high destiny. Let us not miss our calling and our reward because we neglect to love our fellow man and judge them by what we think he should look like on the outside.

God looks at the heart. Men of the world worship outward beauty, but if they find it nothing more than an appearance without a reality in manner and deed, it soon tires them. Outer beauty is nothing more than an ornamental show; the highest beauty is the expression of a good heart and a sweet disposition. The Lord values men and women not by their diamonds, their gold, and their titles, but by the purity of their heart and the helpfulness of their character. The only nobility God recognizes is the truth of the heart and the goodness of the life.

The neighborhood bully could be viewed as someone like Ms. Carson. However, his idea about people is that he should be able to manipulate, harass, and control them. God wants us to love one another, not control each other. The road that he was on as a teenager, if not detoured, could have caused him to grow up to be an abuser of women.

We must speak up and take action; break the silence. We are called to use what we must to assist and serve others. There can be a terrible stigma of shame surrounding those exploited by harassment and abuse. As followers of Christ we have the opportunity to see, treat others right, and speak up for those who for various reasons cannot stand up for themselves. It is imperative that we uphold the dignity of others and respect their worth. They have a voice—it's up to us to help make sure others hear it! The goal is to speak so they get justice—not to speak so we can be heard, for Proverbs 31:8-9 (NIV) says, "Speak up for those who cannot speak for themselves, for the rights of all who are destitute. Speak up and judge fairly; defend the rights of the poor and needy."

We are not only to love God, but also love our fellow man. If you want to be beautiful in your life, you must copy the disposition of Jesus, who lived for one great objective, namely, to bless and save mankind. Whoever lives in love lives in God, and God lives in them.

WHAT SCRIPTURE SAYS ABOUT HOW TO TREAT OTHERS:

John 7:24 (KJV)—"Judge not according to the appearance but judge righteous judgment.

Ephesians 4:2 (NIV)--"Be completely humble and gentle; be patient, bearing with one another in love."

1 Peter 4:8 (NIV)--"Above all, love each other deeply, because love covers over a multitude of sins."

John 15:12 (NIV)--"My command is this: Love each other as I have loved you."

1 Samuel 16:7 (KJV)—"But the Lord said unto Samuel, Look not on his countenance, or on the height of his stature; because I have refused him: for the Lord seeth not as man seeth; for man looketh on the outward appearance, but the Lord looketh on the heart."

Chapter 6: A Butterfly on the Rise

As I headed to high school in 1965, the discussion about civil rights and separate but equal was brewing. My cousin Willie had long since left; he got a job at the grocery store in town as a meat cutter and started a family of his own. My older sisters had grown up and moved on and, with that, Dorthea no longer came to live with us in the summertime. My daddy had left farming behind and gotten a job with the State Department of Transportation, indicating that farming had become too demanding for his aging body. In other words, our family had taken on a completely new dynamic. I was the oldest of the children at home now. Life was good!

We talked a lot about the situation in town and I was paying more attention to how things were. I remember there were two doctors in town who practiced general medicine. Both had two waiting rooms, one for Blacks and one for Whites. There was a café in town that had one serving counter for Blacks and another side that had seating to accommodate the Whites who wanted to sit and eat their food. From my vantage point, there was no difference among people, so why was there unequal treatment? For that matter, I had always wondered why this held true. In school, in church, in businesses, there was always separation. I never could wrap my mind around how there was no fairness in that. I always wondered, but I had not heard the situation discussed to any extent in earlier years or maybe I had not noticed it that much. The leaders in church seemed to become more and more vocal about the situation.

I remember one day we went to town shopping. I got really bold and went to the café to the side labeled "White." I did it, not because I wanted to sit down as much as I wanted to see the difference in what was being served over there; it had to be different, I thought, otherwise why would they serve it from a different side? I found that they were serving the same items on both sides and charging the same prices; it was just that they wanted to keep the races separate. I strolled right in the front door, walked over to the counter, and placed my order. There was a middle-aged White man standing behind the counter. His face turned as red as a beet. He brought his face down so close to mine you would think he was getting ready to kiss me. I kind of stepped back from him, thinking he is in my personal space. He hissed through closed, clinched teeth, "Don't you know, n... are served on the other side? This side is not for colored." I quickly shot back, "My money is green, what color is theirs?" Everybody stopped cold. Nobody said a word and the man behind the counter grew even redder. I felt a real disaster coming on and I knew that I did not, at that point, have a plan B. But just as always, this calm feeling came over me and I could hear this voice, not in my ear, but in my heart say, "Everything is going to be just fine." The Comforter is always here.

At that moment, the owner stepped from behind the swinging door to the kitchen. The owner, incidentally, also owned the fertilizer mill in town. My daddy had brought supplies from him when he was farming for as long as I could remember. He knew exactly who I was. He said, "You are one of those girls of George Martin's, aren't you?" In that moment, I felt it particularly important that I own my own identity, so I spoke right up, "Yes, I am Beverly Martin." I thought that was the best way to get everybody in the place to at least see that I was a person; I had an identity and I was somebody. He walked over to the counter and leaned over and said softly to me, "If you want to buy something, go to the other side and they will serve you." But I knew I had to do something more. I also knew that I couldn't demand they serve me, but my inner self was screaming, YOU HAVE TO DO SOMETHING! Just at that minute, I heard myself saying, "No, thank you. I will take my business elsewhere." Now, what kind of money do you think a young country teenager living in the mid '60s had to spend to take her business elsewhere? With that, I turned and walked out, slamming the door behind me. I felt as if I was 10 feet tall and had just defeated Pharaoh's army. Now, I had a good idea of how David felt when he took Goliath down. And I imagined it felt good, because at that moment I felt REAL good.

When I walked out onto the street, there were several old timers leading against a car parked in front of the cafe and a few others on the street. Their stare of amazement was longer and harder than those of the customers I had just left in the café. The only thing was their stares were for different reasons. One of the men leading on the car was very familiar to me. In fact, he was one of my daddy's friends. He walked over and put his hand on my arm and asked why I was in there and if they had done anything to me. I replayed for him what had happened. He looked back at his friend and laughed, "She's something isn't she? Good for you, Bev. You certainly are your daddy's child." Both stood there with their heads tilted back, laughing as I went off down the street to get with my parents who were at the Main Street department store. As I walked along, pleased with myself, Psalm 138:3 came to mind, and I said, "You made me bold with strength in my soul."

After that day, I pledged to myself to pay attention to the issue of civil rights and, although young, I will wage my own war whenever I got a chance and get involved with others fighting for the cause.

There was a whistle that blew each night at 9 o'clock. That sound signified that the town was closing for the night. Earlier in the week, my father had dropped a bucket of tar on his foot at work. That evening around 8 o'clock he drove to town to get something for the pain. When he got there, it was almost 9 and the stores were about to close. He said he parked the car and hurried as best he could with his injured foot to get into the drug store before the doors were locked. He made his purchase and left the store. He was almost to his car when he heard a voice behind him, "Hey, boy, don't you know the whistle is about to blow? What are you doing still on the street? Are you drunk, straggling like that?" My father said that anger combined with the pain he felt got the best of him. He turned around and told the police officer that he was not drunk, he was on the street because it's a free country and he was not a boy. He could see the officer loosen his billy club from his waist as he came closer. My daddy turned around and continued toward his car. He could hear the officer beat the club against the palm of his hand as he continued. Then he said, "Boy, I believe you are drunk, and I am going to have to take you to jail." My dad said he stopped in his tracks and told the officer again that he was not drunk, but if he hit him with that club, he would have to take him to jail because he was going to handle him for a few minutes, sore foot and all. I didn't know if that changed the officer's mind, but he backed down and said, "OK, now go on and get off the street," and walked away.

Things were beginning to heat up and turbulent times were upon our small southern town as Blacks around the country demonstrated and made their voices heard concerning civil rights and desegregation. The whole country was fired up, including our small town. On an April day in 1968, when I was a junior in high school, the news came that the Rev. Dr. Martin Luther King Jr., the powerful civil rights leader, had been assassinated.

The Civil Rights Era was in full swing. The struggle for social justice that took place mainly for Blacks to gain equal rights under the law in the United States was talked about everywhere. Blacks had had enough of prejudice and violence against them and they wanted an end to legalized racial discrimination, disenfranchisement and racial segregation in this country.

Ironically, it was in that same year that Dr. King was assassinated that separate but equal public schools were ruled unconstitutional, which ushered in freedom of choice. In our town there was a high school for Blacks and a high school for Whites. Students were given a choice of which school they wanted to attend. Of course, none of the White students elected to come across the tracks to our school. However, 12 students from my school were among those who chose to go to the previously all-White school. I was not one of them, although my parents really wanted me to go. I never wanted to be with them; all I wanted was to gain the right to have equal access. That had happened and I was satisfied. I was truly a butterfly on the rise. It was as if something inside of me was telling me, "It's alright now." It was at those times that I knew that my Comforter had been watching over me and fighting the battle invisibly, not only for me but for all who needed a strong warrior.

One of the young men who had chosen to attend the school "across the tracks" talked to me often. He would share with me how the 12 of them were treated and how they had to work harder and be twice as good to gain recognition at that school. They were referred to as the dozen Black specks by some Whites around town. But they were smart, and they always rose to the task. The year after I graduated from high school, incidentally, all schools were desegregated, and we then had just one high school in our town. That is the year when private White academies started popping up all over our county.

GOLDEN NUGGET FOR GROWTH #6

Prejudice, discrimination, and inequality have been around since sin was introduced into the world in the Garden of Eden and slavery was at its base. One vague reference in Genesis chapter four, verse 15, leads some to justify owning slaves — the so-called "Mark of Cain." That reference suggests that God placed a visible "mark" on Cain for murdering his brother and lying about it when God asked what had happened. Cain's curse was therefore interpreted as Black skin, and I guess that is why millions of

Christians have used it to justify slavery. Also, the so-called "Curse of Ham" was another biblical justification some probably used. I gather that much of contemporary racism, discrimination, and prejudice are rooted in those assertions. Throughout different books of the Bible there is evidence of discrimination and inequality.

In society, I believe that every individual has the right to a voice, no matter how small he is, where he is socially, or his standings in society. To me, that is a God-given right. That is how I understand the Scriptures.

It takes moral courage to challenge prejudice and discrimination because preconceived opinions that are not based on reason or actual experience are hard to take down. Situational prejudice and discrimination such as that displayed in the '50s and '60s, and before, were the norm in society passed down from parents, friends, and society and generally learned through living in and observing what was acceptable during the times.

Attitudes toward minorities, especially people of color, have been marked by discrimination historically in this country. Social norms and cultural contexts have always played a significant role in the types of prejudice a person is likely to hold. Racism has figured prominently in American life for centuries. However, that does not make it right. During the fight for equality the federal courts were used to challenge disenfranchisement, segregation, and civil rights for all individuals. Even in 2020, it is not surprising that racial discrimination and prejudices still exist and, as I see it, these feelings are much more prevalent against people of color than many are willing to acknowledge.

Why does anyone see the need to degrade others? Why would anybody want to refuse to mingle with other individuals? Why do some people think that individuals should be rated according to their skin color? These are all WHYs that individuals should not have an answer for if they have belief and faith in a just God who sent his Son to walk among men, suffer and die that ALL might be saved.

Regardless of what others say, Jesus loves all of us deeply and He hurts when we hurt.

The journey to equal rights for all people has been much more difficult and lonelier than it should have been, but as the struggle ensued, we were not alone; God walked every step with us.

No matter what has happened in the past, our past doesn't have to define our future. Our lives have purpose and each of us is significant. None of us are free until we all are free. God is still on the throne! "God shows no partiality."

WHAT SCRIPTURE SAYS ABOUT DISCRIMINATION:

Romans 2:11 (KJV)--"For there is no respect of persons with God."

Ephesians 4:32 (NIV)--"Be kind and compassionate to one another, forgiving each other, just as in Christ, God forgave you."

Luke 6:31 (ESV)--"And as you wish that others would do to you, do so to them."

CHAPTER 7: The Stuff High School Was Made Of

Oh, so much to talk about, so much to do. Those were the buzz words as my high school years progressed. There was an adventure around every turn. I had gotten very attached to a group of my classmates to the point that everyone referred to us as the "Tight Twelve" and we were the "unofficial" leaders in the school's student body. Some who did not care for us referred to us as the "Dirty Dozen." However, there were very few students in the school who looked at us in that light because we were good friends with everybody. Early on, I had grown very fond of one of the members of the Tight Twelve. His name was Shawn. He lived in my neighborhood and we attended the same church. However, after his parents decided to move to town, I mostly saw him at school or at church. Although my parents did allow me to have my friends over on Friday nights (provided they were gone by 9 o'clock), that was not always possible for him. He didn't drive nor was there a car available for him to drive even if he could. Fortunately for me, one of the Tight Twelve, Kirby, had a car, a pink convertible Pontiac. He was generous enough to drive him out some Friday evenings.

One Friday during Study Hall, several of us figured out a way for us to spend time together that weekend. To make it work, the plan could not seem suspicious. A fifth Sunday was coming up, which meant the Sunday School Convention was scheduled at the First Baptist Church in town. We plotted to go out and have some fun after the convention. So, here comes the shady stuff. It was plotting time. I convinced my parents to let me stay over and go home with one of the girlfriends that afternoon. It worked and it was on. After church, we changed at Elizabeth's house and here comes the posse, the T-Twelve. It took two cars to fit all 12 of us; one was the pink Pontiac; and Kirby could really handle that car. His father was a mechanic and he had helped him rebuild it from bumper to bumper. There was never a spot on it and when he drove up and parked in the student parking spaces at school, everybody crowded around, and he would slowly let the top back if it was a sunny day.

We drove out into the county to Perkin's Pond, where there was a pond down near the edge of the woods. It was a great place for swimming, but we did not swim because we were so busy plotting that we forgot all about our swimming gear. We just messed around and had fun all afternoon. We totally lost track of time and before we realized, it was way past the time to be back in town. By the time we got everybody dropped off, it was panic time. Since my parents liked my friend Kirby best, owner of the pink Pontiac, we decided that he would drive me home with Shawn in tow...me sitting in the back seat with Elizabeth and the fellas in front. Anyway, Kirby had always acted older than any of us, although he wasn't. Problem was, parents do not believe anything teenagers tell them, especially when they are in a jam. Even though I had never given my parents any reason to doubt what I said, you still know parents...I should have been home at 5 o'clock.

Kirby said, "When we get to your house, let me do the explaining, because Mr. Martin likes me a lot more than he does Shawn, for obvious reasons, Shawn is your boyfriend." Upon arrival, Kirby had manufactured the most believable lie you could ever imagine. He told my daddy that he ran over a nail and punctured his tire. The spare tire was flat, and everything was closed, so they left us with the car and took the other one across town to his dad's garage to get the air pump. By the time they returned and changed the tire, it was late. He assured my dad, along with Shawn, that it would not happen again. My dad's reply was, "If it does, there won't be another time." Well, we made it through that one, but in the back of my mind I was thinking, "Why didn't we just tell the truth?" After all, we had done nothing wrong, and here we are lying. Did we not learn anything at the Sunday School Convention earlier that day?

I soon forgot that because I was so glad that I had gotten to spend an entire afternoon with Shawn and all my friends. Still, something kept nagging at me and I could hear a little voice in my head repeating James 4:17 (ESV), "Whoever knows the right thing to do and fails to do it, for him it is sin." By the time I got in bed that night, guilt had begun to outweigh the fun memories of that whole afternoon.

Most days, during Study Hall, I worked in the Guidance Office. The T-Twelve had various jobs around school where they assisted. I loved the guidance counselor and all the teachers for that matter. Our principal was a sweetheart and he made being in high school more like an adventure than going to class and doing work. There was one teacher on staff that I simply adored. He was a dream boat. I think all the girls felt the same way about him as I did. There was no funny business or hanky panky going on; he was just easy on the eyes and his personality made it easy to just figuratively fall in love with the idea of falling in love with him. Never in a million years would I have tried to act on it even if he would have wanted to go along with such, and he would never have done anything like that. All the girls fell all over each other to do his assignments and we studied hard to make an A in his class. Yes, high school life was good in the '60s, nothing like today. Everybody looked out for one another and helped one another along the way. But...I didn't say that everything went smoothly all the time.

There was one teacher that was not rated right up there at the top with the others. He was one of the math teachers. He was so predictable and wrong, most of the time. We referred to him as Dr. Jekyll and Mr. Hyde. When we were in class, he always wore a white lab coat; for the life of me I never figured out why. He would start off like Dr. Jekyll and go through the lesson for the day and what he expected us to know at the end of the class. Then he would go to the board and proceed to solve an equation, just as wrong as two left shoes. If someone would question his method or say they don't think the problem is right, Mr. Hyde would come out. I was usually the one who challenged him first. He hated it with a passion. He would sometimes get so mad he would punish the entire class by giving a huge assignment that would be due by the end of class. He always found a way to mark my grades down, because he said that I was the ring leader and tried to make him look bad. Even after much complaining to the principal, our parents, the counselor, and everybody else we could complain to, nothing was really done. He would always have some twist in his test that he could grade subjectively and use it to justify why he gave a certain grade, even though it was a math class. Parents had conferences with him, and the principal had long conversations with him, which never helped. The result would always be that aside from his untactful behavior, he was really in charge of his classroom. My parents would simply tell me, "Go to class, do your work, and don't try to challenge him." That is what we all decided to do and when we didn't understand a problem, we got together at Study Hall or after school and figured it out before we went back to class the next day. However, in my heart, I knew he was wrong;

he was not setting a very good example and he was a lousy teacher. I expected that a lot of us prayed extra prayers for him at night. My Comforter knew he was wrong because I could feel something tugging at my heart strings, assuring me that I was doing the right thing. We got through that class by the Grace of God.

The debate club was the best! We got to travel to other schools with our history teacher, who was the debate team coach. He was a wonderful teacher and coach. I remember one day we went to an away-debate competition and stopped at this little café that had a drive-up window where sandwiches could be ordered. Coach was standing outside his car eating his hot dog while we were setting on the bench in front of the café. He laid his glasses on the top of his car, along with his cup of coffee. We all got into the car and he drove off, and there goes the cup of coffee splashing the hood and rolling off onto the ground and the glasses right behind it. He stopped and luckily although his glasses had coffee on them they otherwise were not damaged. When we got to the other school, before the competition, he said to us, "You all have to win now; after all, I risked my glasses to get you here." We all had a good laugh, but we did win the match.

My junior prom was the biggest event of the season. We had planned for months. My sister and her husband, who lived in Delaware, sent me a beautiful pink lace gown to wear. I had white set-back heeled shoes that were very popular at the time. Shawn's mother had picked out a beautiful corsage and boutonniere for us to wear that matched my dress and his tuxedo with the pink matching cummerbund. We had everything planned out down to who would ride in which car. It was almost D-Day, the day of the prom, and everything was in place. We were in French class and I started seeing black dots before my eyes and my stomach felt like someone was kicking me in my gut. I made it through the day after spending most of it in the bathroom. On the bus that evening, I really got bad and the driver had to leave the highway and drive me down the tree-lined path right up to my front door because I couldn't stand up. My mommy came out all alarmed and one of the fellas on the bus helped her get me in the house. Everybody on the bus was hanging out the window telling me to feel better. They were so afraid that I would not be able to go to the prom the next night. Because my dad was at work, my mommy got the neighbor up the road to drive us to the doctor in town. As we drove up the path to the highway, all I could see were those treetops lining each side of the path and think about those palm trees we had been working on in the gym for the prom scene.

When we reached the doctor's office, there was nobody in the waiting room and the nurse said to bring her on back. He took one look at me and said, "Another one. I have been seeing patients all week with these symptoms." He examined me and I didn't have a temperature. He said that I had a 24-hour virus and should be better in a few days. "A few days!" I yelled. I have to go to prom tomorrow night. The doctor told my mommy that he doubted if I would be feeling well enough to go to the prom. The virus is not life threatening, he said, and that if I take in lots of liquids to stay hydrated, I should be fine. We went home and my mommy gave me chicken soup and told me to drink the broth when I finished, and a large glass of water. As soon as I had finished, it all came back up just as it had gone down. She gave me clear water with baking soda in it and that seemed to help my stomach feel better. I did not try to eat anything else that evening. I got cleaned up, put on my nightgown, and went to bed. All I could think about was the prom that I would surely miss the next night. I prayed as I had never prayed before.

My younger sister came in and said, "Well, I guess all those pretty things you got for the prom were for nothing." I kind of lost my temper and yelled for her to get out and close the door behind her. She said that I forgot that was her room, too. As soon as the harsh words came out of my mouth, I was sorry and told her so. I could feel a rush of calm come over me and my whole body seemed to relax. Shortly afterward, I drifted off to sleep and only woke up around midnight when my mommy came in with a dose of medicine she got from the doctor.

The next morning, I was my old self again. I hopped out of bed and ran in the kitchen and told my mommy that I felt fine. She said, "Well, you are not going to school, just in case." It felt like my whole world had fallen apart. I went back to my bed and covered my head with the pillow and the tears just rolled. After a while, my mommy came in and said she had fixed me breakfast and added that if I could keep it down, she might see about getting me to school at lunch time. Not only did I eat all of it, I kept it down, got myself ready, put on my clothes, and waited. At about 11:30 she said that she knew how much this meant to me and she had gotten the neighbor to take me to school. When I walked out of the front office and started down the hall, the word had gotten around, and the students came running from every direction. The principal had to get on the intercom to bring order back to the halls. All the juniors and seniors who wanted to were dismissed at 2 o'clock to go home and get ready because the decorations were all finished. I was so happy that I didn't even care that I had to stay at school until 3 o'clock for the bus, even though Kirby had offered to drive me home then. God had answered my prayers and I felt well and everything else would fall in place.

That evening when I got home, my mommy curled my hair with the hot curlers, and I looked like a princess in my pink gown. What I had not counted on was Shawn's father taking us. When he drove up and Shawn got out, I almost dropped my teeth. My daddy was smiling. Shawn shrugged his shoulders as he pinned my corsage on and said, "Well what could I do?" Shawn had polished the car so much that I could see myself shine in the door as he opened it and we got into the back seat and his father drove off. I felt like Cinderella going to the ball in my pink gown, beautiful corsage, and Shawn sitting beside me in his black tuxedo and pink cummerbund and boutonniere. We had so much fun and everybody had a good time, even the faculty. As I took my seat after the last dance, I whispered gently as I look up, "Thank you, Lord." I am almost positive that a light twinkled as if to say, "You are welcome."

Shawn's older brother was waiting in the parking lot when the prom was over. Both of us said at the same time, "Thank God for little favors." Everybody was going to the local soda shop for a little while after the prom and we certainly didn't want anyone seeing his father driving us. After-parties were unheard of back then. His brother told us he would wait for us up the street in front of the Laundromat. He leaned out the window as we walked across the street and said, "You can walk on up there when you are ready, but you better not forget Beverly has a curfew." He didn't have to remind us because I want to tell you, I wasn't going to do anything to mess this night up because I was so thankful that I got to go to my first junior-senior prom.

And that is the stuff my high school years were made of.

GOLDEN NUGGET FOR GROWTH #7

In the '60s teenagers mostly placed value on friendship. They were more likely to enjoy spending time with friends and less time around the house. They were bold and adventurous, but a lot more respectful than teens today. More of them could be found in church on Sunday mornings along with family. Although they preferred being with friends, they valued and respected the family institution and traditional religion.

Every generation of teens is shaped by the social, political, and economic events of the day. So, during my teenage generation, teenagers paid attention to civil rights, racial tensions, and other issues current during that time. They were also quick to point out ills and mistreatment inflected by others and felt strongly about adults doing something about those ills. Their lives were centered around each other and having fun, freedom, and liberty, unlike teenagers of today whose lives are saturated by mobile technology, social media, and sex.

Teenagers during that generation didn't have much of an idea which direction their lives would take, and perhaps it may have seemed that they did not care. However, most of the students in my high school were grounded; they knew what they wanted to do with their lives, and they worked hard toward making it happen. Most of all, they cared about each other and had a willingness to hold that sense of community, dear to their hearts.

WHAT SCRIPTURE SAYS ABOUT HOW YOUNG PEOPLE SHOULD LIVE:

Ephesians 6:4 (ESV)--"Fathers, do not provoke your children to anger, but bring them up in the discipline and instruction of the Lord."

Psalm 119:9 (ESV)--"How can a young man keep his way pure? By guarding it according to your word."

1 Timothy 4:12 (ESV)--"Let no one despise you for your youth, but set the believers an example in speech, in conduct, in love, in faith, in purity."

Proverbs 1:8-9 (ESV)--"Hear, my son, your father's instruction, and forsake not your mother's teaching, for they are a graceful garland for your head and pendants for your neck."

CHAPTER 8: As Time Passed On

In the summer of 1968 after my junior year in high school, I went to Delaware to stay with one of my older sisters for the summer. We drove up in my daddy's new car that he had just gotten (well, it wasn't new; it was used, but new to us). It was nice and roomy and had plenty of space in the back seat for my two younger sisters, my brother, and me. We got there late on a Friday afternoon and had a wonderful weekend. We went to the beach that Saturday and I got a terrible sunburn. My mommy said it was because I didn't listen and put on the sun screen evenly and wouldn't spend any time under the beach umbrella. Of course, I didn't agree with that and had my own ideas about why I got too much tan.

My parents and siblings left about mid-day on Sunday. I had written Shawn a long letter that I was going to give to my younger sister to mail when she got home, but I decided against that because it was too personal and I knew she would open and read it. I had only gotten to talk to him one time since school closed for the summer and then for a few minutes just before we left on Friday. As my parents and siblings drove away that Sunday afternoon, I started planning what I would do with my summer. I knew that if I did not keep busy, I would get homesick, not so much because I wanted to be at home, but because I would miss the T-Twelve and especially Shawn. I had already braced myself to get used to missing him and the summer had not even started. I dropped the letter in the mail that Monday afternoon.

During the day, I didn't have much to do because my sister and her husband were at work and the children were in day care. I offered to babysit them, but my sister said they were too much of a handful and I needed to enjoy myself. After that first week, I was tired of reading, watching television, and walking to the strip mall a few blocks away. My sister got an idea one Saturday afternoon when we were at the amusement park. She asked me how I would like to have a job. I thought it was a wonderful idea. One of her co-worker's husband owned a drug store in the neighborhood and he needed part-time help at the soda counter. I got the job and enjoyed every minute of it. It was less like work and more like social hour every day. It was the neighborhood teenager hangout and I got to be friends with most of them. Sometimes, on my days off, a group of us would go to the amusement park or to the movies. We always went swimming on Sunday afternoon at the city pool.

When summer was over and it was time to go home, I kinda dreaded having to leave. My sister had a small going-home party for me and invited some of the new friends I had made. I wanted to stay, and they all envied me because I lived in the rural South where they wanted to live. Shawn had never answered the letter I wrote him at the beginning of the summer, and I had not talked to him. I was sad at first, but after I met new friends, I was fine. I came home on a Tuesday. When the Greyhound bus pulled into the bus station on Main Street in town, it seemed like another world. The first familiar thing I saw was Kirby's pink Pontiac parked across the street. He slid out of the car and ran across in front of the slow-moving cars as I walked away from the bus to the covered porch area with a suitcase in each hand. I was happy to see him, and I dropped the suitcases and we hugged for a long time. He sat with me while I waited for my daddy to come pick me up. We talked about how our summers had gone and I asked him if he had seen Shawn. He acted as if he didn't want to talk about Shawn. Then as he kicked a bottle top on the ground, he said, "I bet Shawn would have been standing here if he had known you were coming today." I asked him why he was here, and his answer surprised me. He said, "Oh, I just had a feeling that you were going to be on this 3 o'clock bus." Soon after that, my daddy arrived, and we said our goodbyes and I got in my daddy's car. As we drove away, I yelled, "Be sure to tell Shawn I am home, if you see him." He didn't acknowledge that he had heard me. Later, I would find out why.

When I got home and got all settled in and showed my mommy the new things I had bought, I went out and sat on the porch. I kept looking down the tree-lined path hoping to see a car coming with Shawn in it. Surely, Kirby had told him that I was home by now. I went in and picked up the phone; it was busy (we were on a party line, a shared telephone service back then). I went back on the porch and thought to myself that I knew it was a reason that the line was busy. I don't need to be the first to call; after all, he went all summer without even trying to reach me, not once!

That Wednesday night, we went to Bible Study. It had not gotten dark yet, so some of us teenagers were still hanging back outside before going into class. There was no sign of Shawn or any of the usual gang. Then one of the girls from school said to me, "Did you hear about Shawn and Kirby?" I asked, "What about them?" "Well," she said but then she hesitated. "I guess I will let them tell you." I grabbed her arm and said, "I know you don't think you are going in before you finish telling me what you started." With reservation, she told me that they had a big fight (verbal) about me just after I left for the summer. "Kirby told Shawn that he cares more for you than he did," she said. Shawn shot back, "I knew it all along and she would probably pick you over me if it came down to it." I couldn't believe two of the T-Twelve were fighting and about me of all things. For the remainder of the evening, I could think of nothing else. When we got home, I was quiet and didn't even watch television. I went straight to bed. I was hoping that I would get that feeling that I always got when I needed reassurance. It did not come, and I soon fell asleep.

The next day, I asked if I could go to Elizabeth's house in town. She had her license by now and her parents trusted her to drive out in the country. I called her and she came later in the day. My mommy said I could stay until my daddy got home from work and he would pick me up. I could not wait to get in the car with Elizabeth. She said, "Child, some things have been going on this summer." It turned out that Kirby confessed to Shawn that he was in love with me. I never had any idea! Once we got to her house, she told me the whole story. She also said that she saw Shawn earlier before she left to pick me up and told him that I would be at her house later. Pretty soon, Shawn came walking up the street. We were sitting on the porch and he came up and leaned against the banister. I wanted to run to him, but I was confused and didn't know what to do. He finally said, "I guess you heard what happened with Kirby and me." All I could think of to say was, "No, I want to hear it from you." Elizabeth knew that was her cue to leave, so she said she would go and fix us some Kool-Aid, and she disappeared into the house.

Shawn came up and sat in a chair across from me; he then got up and kissed me on the cheek. He sat back down and dropped his head. He told me that he was sorry about everything that had happened and that we all had been friends for such a long time. But he sensed that Kirby was really "stuck" on me and he valued both of us as his best friends and he wanted to remain our best friends instead of Kirby's rival. I eventually found voice enough to say, "What do you mean?" He answered by saying that he wanted us to be friends not boyfriend and girlfriend. He had felt that way for a long time and he knew if we couldn't be just friends, we would lose everything else we had. He said that even before Kirby admitted to him that he cared about me, he already knew.

Well, with me being the person I am, I told Shawn that if that is the way he wanted it, that was fine with me and I would always be his friend no matter what. Elizabeth returned with the drinks and I held the iced glass up to my face pretending to cool off, but I was really trying to disguise the tears that had started to run down my face. To this day, I cannot remember if they were sad tears or tears of relief. Shawn turned and walked away. He looked back over his shoulder and said he would see us later and that he needed to go clear his head. Elizabeth and I pondered over the situation all afternoon, first on the porch, then in her room, then down the street. We walked up to the Tastee Freez and a few of the T-Twelve were there, including Kirby. We made polite conversation about the summer in town and my summer in Delaware…no mention of Kirby and Shawn. I couldn't look at Kirby and he couldn't look at me. Everybody knew what had happened. Finally, someone asked if anybody had seen Shawn today. Elizabeth hesitantly admitted, "Yes, he was at my house earlier in the afternoon." Everybody got silent for a long while before we started talking about how glad we were about becoming seniors next week when school starts again.

On the way home in the car, my daddy asked what was wrong. I should have been happy to see my friends again after a long summer. I didn't respond, partly because my mind was a thousand miles away and partly because I felt like I would burst into tears if I said one word. He continued by saying he had not seen Shawn at church lately but had seen him a few times in town during the summer. He laughed, saying he always runs like a rabbit when he sees me as if he's afraid of me. "Now you take that Kirby fella," my daddy said. "He is a mature young man and he is ambitious, helping his daddy at the garage and all. Every time I see him, he stops and has a conversation with me. He asked about you all summer…has so many manners," my daddy said. "Now, I'm not saying Shawn is not a nice young man," he continued. "I'm just saying…." His voice trailed off. I looked at him and gave him a half smile

All through dinner I was quiet and just couldn't sort out my feelings. I moped around the house picking up things then putting them down until it was time to go to bed. I just didn't have the desire to fight for my feelings. I guess I was just as tangled up and twisted as Shawn and Kirby. I did think of one thing my grandmother once said to me, which was, "No matter how inadequate you feel, you can always look to God for help." When I finally went to bed, my eyes became so heavy, it felt like a weight had been lifted from my shoulder. I recognized that feeling and I went right to sleep.

Next morning, I got up with my childhood friend, Estheree, on my mind. I had not talked to her for a long time, but somehow something deep inside was telling me it was time. I could figure out anything with her. God may not come when you want Him, but He is always right on time, because that very day we drove to the big city to buy new clothes for school. As we were walking into Belk-Leggett, the first person I saw was Estheree, walking along with her aunt and grandmother. We hugged each other so hard that I thought I had broken my shoulder. When we finished shopping, I met back up with her for a little while. I told her all about my situation. She shot back at me. "All of this is simple," she said. "I could tell the last time we talked that you cared about Kirby more than you were admitting. Shawn just caught on and decided to make everything right." I had to admit, she was dead on right, just like always. I did value Shawn as a very good friend, but I also felt something quite different for Kirby.

We talked again several times before the opening of school the next week and I promised to let her know what happened when we went back to school. She also told me that she would be going to the former all-White high school on the other side of the county this year. I couldn't understand why she wanted to do it in her senior year, but she said that it would boost her college applications as she wanted to go to a really good college. Then her voice trailed off. "You know my current high school does not have a good academic track record, but if I were applying on an athletic scholarship, I wouldn't have anything to worry about." I did agree with that. Estheree's high school had the best basketball, baseball, football, and track teams in the state.

As I waited in anticipation for the opening of school for my last year, I was not especially eager for that first day to come. There was so much to deal with, so many emotions festering and changing of feelings and of hearts. I did what I had become accustomed to doing, prayed for guidance and assurance. My Comforter had never failed me yet. This time I wondered if it would be that simple. But as time passes on, we find a way to figure it all out.

GOLDEN NUGGET FOR GROWTH #8

We see new people every day, and we get to know others so well that it seems that we have known them for a lifetime but, too often, we don't see them for who they really are and therefore don't really know them at all. Our vision of them is so clouded that we can't see that they are human beings capable of doing marvelous things. This is true because when we spend too much time focusing on ourselves, we overlook the qualities in others.

We need to notice people for who they are and look at them the way God looks at them. It is so easy to become wrapped up in making your own life shiny and bright that you can't see the forest for the trees. Sometimes, we are so dedicated to holding a friendship together that we risk our own happiness to save that friendship. The best thing we can do is stop spending so much time looking out the window and spend more time looking in the mirror. If we would just do that, we can see what others really mean to us and understand that we owe them much more than we have given. Love and forgiveness walk hand in hand in a relationship. As James 2:17 (NIV) suggests, "People who don't help those in need show that their faith may be dead." James again writes that "faith by itself, if it is not accompanied by action, is dead." The action you take after you screw up, is really what defines who you are.

WHAT SCRIPTURE SAYS ABOUT LOVE AND FRIENDSHIP:

Proverbs 17:9--"Love prospers when a fault is forgiven, but dwelling on it separates close friends."

Colossians 3:14 (NIV)--"And over all these virtues put on love, which binds them all together in perfect unity."

1 Thessalonians 3:12 (NIV)--"May the Lord make your love increase and overflow for each other and for everyone else, just as ours does for you."

Colossians 3:13 (NIV)--"Bear with each other and forgive one another if any of you has a grievance against someone. Forgive as the Lord forgave you."

1 Corinthians 16:14 (NIV)--"Do everything in love."

Chapter 9: Twelve Beautiful Relationships Coming to an End

The first day of my senior year in high school was not at all how I had imagined it over the years. It was the end of summer 1968. I was anxious and for the first time since grade school, I was at a loss for words or a sense of how to handle a touchy situation. On the bus ride to school, I was deep in thought wondering why Shawn and Kirby had made such bold moves. They were best friends and true friends are friends for life. It seemed as if my thoughts were coming from my heart instead of my head saying, "Can't you understand, they admitted the truth to each other because they ARE friends." As the bus pulled up in front of the gym to unload, the first person I saw at the flagpole raising the flag was Shawn. Kirby's pink Pontiac was parked in the student lot alongside several other cars, so I knew he was somewhere nearby.

After unloading the bus, I walked slowly down the sidewalk looking straight ahead. Elizabeth came running out of the building to meet me. She was all excited and boasting about how this would really be our year. As the "take in" bell sounded, we all crowded inside the gym waiting for assignments for homeroom. The three classes of seniors were called first. To my surprise, all 12 of us were in the same homeroom and Mr. Dream Boat, whom all the girls adored, was our homeroom teacher. Elizabeth ended up seated in the row on one side of me and Shawn on the other side, opposite me. I cut my eye and Kirby was sitting in the back of the room. Almost as soon as we were seated, Shawn shot a folded note in what seemed like a million pieces over to my desk. I opened it just as the teacher started to talk. When I looked up, he was standing right beside my desk. I was horrified when he asked, "Ms. Martin, would you like for me to wait until you finish, or would you like to share that with the class?" I crumpled the piece of paper up and shoved it into my purse. I thought to myself, is this the way the school year is going to be?

I read the note between classes and Shawn wanted to talk to me alone. I knew that would be impossible at school because the T-Twelve were always together, but with Kirby and Shawn at odds, I did not know how this would play out. It seemed as if all the others knew something that I was not privy to because at lunch time, everybody scattered when Shawn walked up to the table with his tray. He asked if I minded if he sat with me, and then sat down without waiting for an answer. We talked most of lunch period but did not touch our food. He made me realize something that I was clueless about. He told me that my friendship meant a lot more to him than I realized and that he could not be my boyfriend and my best friend at the same time. It made him uncomfortable with me and the others to be together as my boyfriend. He said he realized what the problem was while I was away during the summer and after Kirby confessed to him that he wanted to be more than a friend to me, he knew our dating had to end. Kirby wanted to let it ride but he thought it was the right thing to do. He also told me that the day on Elizabeth's front porch was the hardest day of his life, but as he walked away, it felt like the weight of the world had been lifted from his shoulder. That was his confirmation that he had made the right decision.

I reassured him that if he and Kirby were OK, then I was also. I pointed out to him that we were still teenagers with our whole lives ahead of us and we should not waste these beautiful years on these weighty problems that really did not make sense. I also assured him that we would be friends for life, no matter what happened. We hugged and went back to class. I felt so much better after we had talked. That afternoon, when he boarded my bus, I was puzzled, because he lived down the street from the school. He picked up my books and purse and slid into the seat beside me, holding my belongings in his lap. He leaned over and said, "Not to worry, I am just riding home with a friend. Bus driver Jeff will let me off when he finishes the bus route and get back to town," he said. We talked about a lot of things before the bus got to my path. As I walked down the tree-lined path home, I felt relief, peace, and serenity--the kind you feel when you are with a genuine friend. It was then that I knew things were going to be alright with us. I threw my purse across my shoulder and strolled on down the path to my house.

Day in and day out, the 12 of us went on being friends. Nobody mentioned the situation between Shawn and me again. There didn't even seem to be a strain between him and Kirby. On occasions, Kirby would even drive me home after school and asked me to go to the movies with him several times; however, we never committed to dating. My younger brother asked at the dinner table one evening, "Why are you always riding with Kirby? I thought you were Shawn's girl." I tried to cut him off, but then I thought...the truth will set you free. I said, "I am nobody's girl. Both Shawn and Kirby are exceptionally good friends of mine. We all will be friends for life, but in the meantime, we have a whole lifetime to figure that out." My dad smiled. If I had to read his mind, I bet he was thinking of how glad he was to hear that.

Fall came and Kirby was elected Student Government Association president and Shawn was elected president of the senior class. Elizabeth was voted homecoming queen and I became Miss Borden High School. The T-Twelve were thicker than thieves and Shawn and I were so much more relaxed around our friends now than when we were dating. I got my driver's license that fall, and my daddy let me drive the car often. I spent a lot more time with Estheree, now that I could drive to her house. She was becoming more like the 13th member of the T-Twelve. Sometimes, when we had a game or some other activity on Friday nights, I would spend the night at my sister's house who lived in town. She was a teacher at the elementary school. On those days, I was supposed to walk home because she lived in town off the bus route. But Jeff would let me ride the bus from school and when we got to the railroad tracks, I would get off and run the tracks for the driver to make sure the train was not coming (that was one of the bus safety procedures); the bus would keep going once it crossed the tracks and I would walk on down the street to my sister's house. After we finished semester exams, we were excited because Christmas was just around the corner and we were about to get out of school for winter break. Estheree and Elizabeth both had boyfriends now that they were serious about. As for me, the notion had left me completely. Estheree would often say, "You would have one, too, if you would just tell Kirby that you feel the same way about him that he feels about you." I never did because I didn't really know how I felt myself.

My sister who lived in New York (Miss Meanie) came home for the holidays the day after we got out of school for Christmas. Now that she was a grown-up, she was not so mean anymore. Go figure. I was glad she was home and we had a wonderful time. We could go shopping and any place we needed to go and stay as long as we wanted because we didn't have to drive my daddy's car. She had her own, a little green convertible Malibu. One evening, we were decorating the Christmas tree and she asked me about my friends. I told her about Shawn and Kirby. She stopped and sat down on the coach, threw her head back, and started laughing. Frankly, I thought she had lost it. Then she said, "I know exactly how all of you feel because I've been there and done that." She told me about the time when she was in sixth or seventh grade back at the old Rosenwald School and what she went through. I vaguely remember that, but I was so young, probably in first or second grade. All I know is that a group of us would be walking home from school and she would fight Wesley James every day; no, let me correct that, she would beat up on Wesley James every day. She was on punishment every evening and she would do the same thing again the next day. My mommy even made her sit beside him through the entire service one Sunday, hoping that would make them get along better. It did not work

My sister went on to explain to me that it's awkward to be friends with peers and date them at the same time because it is too complicated and hard. She told me that she really liked Wesley James as a boyfriend, but she wanted to be his friend, too. Everyday things would turn out wrong and they would have a battle royal, as she put it. "Why do you think he never hit me back?" she asked. I told her that back then I just thought she was being a bully, because she was always bullying me at home. She said that, in truth, she had a huge crush on him and just did not know how to deal with it. He liked her, too, all through high school but they never admitted it. She confessed that as the years passed, she finally got over him. In fact, she told me that he lives in Brooklyn now and works for an advertising agency. Their paths have crossed several times since she has been living in New York, but the flames are dead. They have small talk and go on their way. We both know now that when you are young and immature, you can't cope with certain issues that come up in your life, she said.

We had a wonderful Christmas and she got to meet my friends, all of them. She finally met the T-Twelve plus one. She could not believe that Estheree had grown into such an attractive young lady. What I could not believe is that both Shawn and Kirby gave me the exact same gift for Christmas; a gold locket with the phrase "T-Twelve Forever." I still wonder today if they actually got together and planned that. In my sister's opinion, we acted much more grown-up and dressed more like adults than her class did when they were seniors in high school. Coming from her, that was a real compliment. Yes, the holidays were good and good times just went on and on.

After Christmas dinner, my family was sitting around the living room talking about when we were growing up. The whole family was together for the first time in many years, my parents, younger siblings, my sister and her family from Delaware, my sister and her husband who lived in town, my sister from New York, even Dorthea and my uncle were there. Dorthea's mother and my grandmother had passed away by that time. I looked around and everybody was smiling. I thought to myself I don't know what they are thinking right now, but I am thanking God for blessing me with a family like this. Just as that familiar warm feeling was welling up in my heart, my daddy yelled out, let's gather around the piano and sing some Christmas carols. My daddy was great on the piano. He used to play for the senior choir at church until he decided it was time to let a younger musician take over. One of my older sisters said, "Bev, you just hum because you cannot carry a tune in a bucket." I shot back jokingly, "Well, I might not be able to sing, but you cannot hold a candle to me in anything else I do."

After Christmas break, everybody settled back into their routine. We were all busy checking out and applying to different colleges and stressing over the SATs. All of us wanted to go off to college, but nobody really wanted to leave home. Things even changed at my house. My mother went to work part time at the bakery that had recently opened in town. She had never worked outside the home before and it was kind of weird for her to be leaving home in the morning when we were leaving for school. She said she had time on her hands now that my younger siblings were older and could do things for themselves. Daddy thought it was unnecessary and told her she just needed to get a hobby, but he didn't really care, as long as he had those delicious meals for dinner every night.

My sister who lived in New York came back to visit for a few days in February, on her way back home from a business trip. At that time, she was an accountant for a large company in New York. That night, I had college information laid out on the table. I had picked about five to apply to when she came in and sat down. I asked her if she had this much trouble trying to decide which college she wanted to attend. She said, "Mommy and I decided on two and I went to the one that gave me the most money. So that is where I went," she said. "With the grades you have, you can pick and choose because I am sure you can get a full scholarship from a number of schools," she continued. Then she got a bright idea. "Why don't you apply to Columbia? After all, it is a very prestigious university. Then you can live with me." I had not even thought about a school like Columbia and staying with her was out of the question, I thought to myself. When she got back home, she sent me information about Columbia. After looking at some of the requirements, I had doubts about my chances of even being accepted there. After all, it is an Ivy League school. Then I remembered what James 1:6 (NIV) says, "...the one who doubts is like a wave of the sea that is driven and tossed by the wind." I quickly said, "Why not? Because I can do all things through Christ who strengthens me."

After several weeks of pondering and discussing with my parents and the school guidance counselor, I applied to three more schools and, yes, Columbia University in New York was one of them. At that point, my parents stopped me, citing that the application fees were mounting up as I applied to so many colleges. I was smart and had nearly a 4.0 GPA (would have had a perfect 4.0, if I had not had to deal with Dr. Jekyll and Hyde), so I felt good about my choices and I also had faith. Most of my friends, although brilliant academically, stuck to applying to smaller colleges near home, thinking students from a small town like Coltonville, Georgia, cannot compete in those "high powered" universities

It was one day in late spring of 1969 when I got my SAT scores. I was blown away...I could not believe it. Never in a million years did I think I would score that well. My daddy, as he always did, said jokingly, "I don't know why you are so surprised; after all, you are a Martin aren't you?" I could not wait to share the news with everybody. The next day the guidance counselor announced over the intercom that 22 students had outstanding scores on the SAT. However, the most exciting part was that Shawn had landed an almost perfect score. That Friday afternoon, the principal let the senior advisers sponsor a sock hop in honor of our victory. We had a wonderful time. We all went out to Perkin's Pond after school and I spent the night at my sister's house in town. Yes, 1969 was our year, but it was fast winding down to the end. We would soon be out of school and on our own as adults. We all knew that soon,

12 beautiful relationships would come to an end and, quite possibly, some of us may never see each other again.

I got accepted to most every college I had applied to and was offered full scholarships to some of those. Although I always thought anything is possible, I was still shocked when I got the acceptance letter from Columbia University. I got right on the phone and told my sister in New York the good news. Our nosy neighbor, who was always listening in on everybody's conversations on the party line, yelled louder than my sister when I announced the news. My sister asked, "Is that Mommy on the phone with you?" I did not answer and told her I would talk to her later. For a little while, Columbia, Clemson, and Spelman were at the top of my list, but after talking with my parents, we decided that Columbia was probably not the best choice for me. I finally settled on Clemson University. Without even discussing my decision with her, I found out the same day that Estheree and her grandmother had decided on Clemson, too.

As I lay in bed that night, I thought to myself, what an awesome God. He has a way of making things fall right in place. It was at that time that I knew without a doubt the T-Twelve plus one would be alright, even if we never saw each other again. Anyway, I felt good because I would have my REAL best friend for life, Estheree, right by my side. God has seen to that!

Everybody should have something to believe in; mine is a living, all-knowing, all- powerful, God. We should let our lives reflect the faith we have in God, fearing not the things of the world, and praying about everything. If we just be strong and trust God's Word, in His time, He will be right on time. I agree with Shannon L. Alder, the inspirational author and writer who once said, "Fear is the glue that keeps you stuck. Faith is the solvent that sets you free." As Christians, if we rely on God and look to Him in everything with a God-fearing heart, and through faith our difficulties are resolved. Only if we believe in God's omnipotence, are we able to truly depend on Him. We should have a genuine fellowship with God in everything; especially when trials befall us.

Throughout my own childhood, my adolescence, and later in my teen life, it was proven that if one keeps the faith and stays grounded in what is right, God will resolve the problems and settle concerns as well as provide just what is needed. My early life was not always easy, but it was a piece of cake compared with what some teenagers have to deal. I do know that I had to have a genuine fellowship with God in everything because His power is everywhere.

WHAT SCRIPTURE SAYS ABOUT TRUSTING AND BELIEVING IN GOD:

Psalm 46:1-3 (NIV)--"God is our refuge and strength, an ever-present help in trouble."

Proverbs 18:10 (NKJV)--"The name of the Lord is a strong tower; the righteous run into it and are safe."

Nehemiah 8:10 (NIV)--"Do not grieve, for the joy of the Lord is your strength."

Psalm 9:9 (NIV)--"The LORD also will be a stronghold for the oppressed, A stronghold in times of trouble."

Psalm 18:2 (NIV)--"The LORD is my rock and my fortress and my deliverer, My God, my rock, in whom I take refuge; My shield and the horn of my salvation, my stronghold."

Psalm 37:39 (KJV)--"But the salvation of the righteous is from the LORD; He is their strength in time of trouble."

Psalm 55:22 (NIV)--"Cast your burden upon the LORD and He will sustain you; He will never let the righteous to be shaken."

Psalm 56:3-4 (NIV)--"When I am afraid, I will put my trust in You. In God, whose word I praise, In God I have put my trust; and am not be afraid. What can mortals do to me?"

CHAPTER 10: Off to a Bold New World

Graduation was upon us! Our baccalaureate service was sad but wonderful. The pastor of the First Baptist Church in town delivered the message. There wasn't a dry eye among the seniors or most of the parents. The pastor laid it right on the line as to what we should focus on as we walk out into the bold new world. Near the end of the service, the guidance counselor announced that 47 of the 81 graduating seniors had been accepted to college and 11 of those had received full scholarships. I was one of the 11. My class was proud, girls in their sky-blue dresses and boys in their dark suits. When the glee club members rose and joined the choir on stage to sing the closing song, I sat there mouthing the words along with them, for I knew I dared not try to sing...that would have been hilarious.

Four days later came commencement exercises. Shawn was valedictorian and Wanda Epps, the quietest member of the senior class, was salutatorian. Shawn was remarkable. If he wasn't standing right there at the microphone, it would have been hard to believe that those words were coming from a 17-year-old's mouth. I knew he had been working on the speech for weeks and would not let anyone see it, but I had no idea that it was that good or would be so well delivered. Wanda's speech was good also, but you could tell that she was extremely nervous. I kept whispering under my breath the entire time she was speaking, "Lord, get her through this." She was very shy, and I never heard her say more than two words at one time outside of class. She was going to Shaw University in North Carolina, which was no surprise because all her family went there. One of her uncles even went to Shaw Divinity School. He was a pastor in the city.

After graduation, everybody stayed around for a few days and then they began to scatter. But before they all left, we got together one more time at our usual hangout spot, Perkin's Pond. Kirby left two days later, as he was the only one of the T-Twelve not going to college. He enlisted in the U.S. Navy, something he always wanted to do. Shawn went to work at the beach for the summer before leaving for Nashville, Tennessee, to attend Fisk University. Estheree got a summer job, supervising a summer program, funded by the Borden County School System. Because I planned to major in biology and eventually go into research, the guidance counselor had helped me land an internship at a biomedical research company. It had just moved its headquarters to Research Triangle Park in Durham, North Carolina. At the time it seemed like a long way from home.

I was home for about a week visiting with my friends before my parents packed me up for the trip to North Carolina and my summer job. My mommy was upset, and I thought she would never stop crying after they got me settled and prepared to head back home. She kept telling my daddy, "This is not like spending the summer with one of her sisters in the city. She will be here all by herself, making adult decisions," which was not entirely true, because the company had an agreement with one of the most prestigious universities in Durham for the interns to stay in a dorm on the campus and there were three adult mentors living in the dorm with us.

The four-week internship went fast, and I learned a lot. I still had time to go home and do some things before going to freshman orientation at Clemson. Shawn called a couple of times and I got a long letter from Kirby. I could tell that he missed being at home. I read every word slowly, taking in everything and reading between the lines for things he was not just openly saying. He told me that I could drive his car while I was home if I wanted to; his father wouldn't mind. But I did not think that was a good idea. He gave me every detail about what Navy boot camp was like. He was stationed, at Recruit Training Command Great Lakes, Illinois. He said the first few days were not too challenging; however, after that it became quite testy with push-ups, curl-ups, and either running or swimming, and swimming was not an option. After his seven weeks of boot camp and graduation, he would not get leave, but he would have to travel to his next training location, at what they called A School.

I felt sorry for him and I shared the information with my father. He assured me that it was not as dismal as it sounded. He reminded me that Kirby was a man when he left and being in the Navy was his dream. "Don't worry," he said. "That young man will be just fine." I wrote him back right away, but I waited a few days before I mailed it because I did not want him to think I was too eager.

When it came time to go off to college, I was not ready, but at the same time I was excited. My father arranged for Estheree and me to travel together. He rented a van, packed our belongings in the back, and off we went to Clemson, South Carolina. My daddy and mommy in front, Estheree's aunt in the second row, and the two of us giggling in the third row with bags all around us.

We were roommates and that was a good thing because unlike most of the students there, we knew each other and could share things. So, it was not necessary for us to take two of everything that we needed. We were a good support system for each other, but I was still homesick. I really do believe that if I had gone home the first two weeks, I would not have returned. However, it got better because I stayed on my knees a lot. God will bear your burdens if you just take them to Him and leave them there.

Once we were settled in class and started mingling with the other students, things fell into place. Most evenings, right after returning from the dining hall, Estheree would drag a chair to the phone down the hall from our dorm room and talk to her boyfriend. He was attending Virginia Union University in Virginia. When she finished, we would study until midnight. I looked forward to our studying together because I didn't have anything else to occupy my time like she did. In hindsight, I am glad that I didn't have any love interests. It seemed that her love life drained her.

Toward the end of the first semester, it seemed that something was weighing heavily on my heart and I just could not figure it out. One Sunday morning when we went to the morning service in the Student Union, I realized what it was. The words in the sermon rang so clear that one would have to be asleep to not understand. Through the chaplain's sermon, I realized that the Lord was talking to me. I sat right up in my seat and looked straight ahead as if I expected to see Jesus himself standing there beside the preacher. A little voice was saying to me, "You have your whole life ahead of you and you don't have to live it all today. Take your time and consider what is right and then move ahead." Most of my life I had tried to put all aspects of me and everybody around me into little lock-step compartments and keep them neatly in place as I perceived everything to be, all at once. However, life is not like that. Life is sometimes messy, life is sometimes unpleasant, and life is sometimes unpredictable, but if you trust in the Lord, life can be joyous. You must just live it and have faith that God is going to keep you on the right path if you ask Him to help you.

I looked down and a warm tear had run down my face and fell squarely in the middle of the open page of my Bible. I must have said out loud, "Yes, Lord, I hear you!" because several students turned and looked at me with a smile. Estheree put one arm around my shoulder and said, "I know, I know, you are homesick, aren't you? Trust me, everything will be alright," she continued. I did not say a word, but she could not have been more mistaken in her assumption of why I was shedding tears.

That afternoon after brunch, I went back to the dorm and wrote my parents a note. I told them that things were alright and not to worry about me. I wrote my sister in New York a letter and told her that I had forgiven her for everything she had ever done to me when we were growing up and that I loved her very much. I wrote each of my other older sisters a letter and told them that I appreciated everything they had ever done for me. I wrote Alice, the student in my middle-school class, a letter and told her I was sorry that I didn't get to know her better so I could have been more of a support to her during her illness (knowing that I would never mail that one because I didn't know where to send it). I wrote Shawn a letter and told him that I hoped he was having a successful ime at school and that I missed talking to him and being with him. Finally, I took out fresh stationery that I had been saving for something special and wrote Kirby a letter. I told him that I admired his spirit and his maturity and that I wish I had those qualities. I went on to tell him that I loved him and missed him very much, but we could never be anything more than we are because I was not willing to sacrifice him as a friend for a love affair. When Estheree came in from the canteen, I told her how much I appreciated her as a friend and that she was the best friend I had and, no matter what, I would always be there for her.

Estheree paused for a minute, then she asked me why I was acting so strange. I did not answer. I just looked out the window. She told me that I had nothing to worry about because I was stuck with her for life. Then she spied the pile of letters on my desk, she walked over, and picked them up. The letter to Kirby was on top. She put her arm around me and said, "That's my girl. You are finally telling him how you feel." I asked her what made her come to that conclusion. She ran her finger over the envelope, "Well, this special stationery is a dead giveaway." In the next breath she asked when I had written all those letters. Over time, I said, over time.

Christmas break came, we went home and nothing remarkable happened. I didn't see a lot of my friends. I guess they were doing the same thing I was, spending time with their families.

One day I went to town on an errand from my mommy. When turned on Main Street, I saw the pink Pontiac parked in front of the jewelry store. I froze, thinking to myself when had he gotten home I did not want to face Kirby today. Not after I wrote him that last letter...too much explaining to do, and I was not prepared. Just at that moment, his older brother came out of the store with a small bag in his hand and got in the car. I breathed a sigh of relief and drove on down the street.

Well, 1969 came to a peaceful end and I went back to school happy in January.

When I came home for spring break, Elizabeth was also home. Everybody else seemed to have gone to the beach to unwind because there was nobody in town. Estheree, Elizabeth and I got together one day and drove into the city. It wasn't an especially long drive, but we were in no hurry, so we took our time stopping for gas, then for a soda, then to check out some scarves at a roadside vendor. While we were driving, Elizabeth told us that she had taken her mother to Kirby's parents' house the day before and she heard that he had recently been home on shore leave. His mother said that he loved being in the Navy. I got quiet for a minute, then I was happy for him because he was doing what he had always wanted to do.

That summer, I decided that I needed some me time and did not work. Estheree got her job back from last summer. My sister in New York asked if I wanted to come up and spend a couple of weeks with her. So, I did. I boarded the Greyhound bus at the station in town and off I went. When I got to Baltimore, I had to get a connecting bus to go on to the Port Authority Terminal in New York City. I was walking along the platform with suitcase in tow when I heard a tap on the window. I looked up and there was Shawn with a big smile on his face. I boarded the bus, he put my suitcase up top, and I took the seat beside him. First thing he asked was where I was going. I told him and he said that he was going to Atlantic City to meet several of his friends from school. One of them lived in Atlantic City and had gotten jobs for them there for the summer. The bus was getting crowded. I saw Shawn when he turned his class ring around to make it look like a wedding band so people would think we were married. That would give him more of a legitimate reason for not giving up his seat to anybody. I punched him in the arm and said smiling, "You know you're wrong." As the bus pulled out from Baltimore, we started covering everything that had happened the previous year. I mean everything. He told me that he had talked to Kirby several times on the phone and he seemed to be holding down the Navy. We both had a good laugh from that.

During the two weeks I spent with my sister, Shawn came over once and she took us to a nice restaurant near Central Park. We had a good time and he stayed the night, on the couch, of course. After that, my sister drove me back home and I spent the remainder of the summer uneventfully. We went to the beach several times, spent some time with my younger siblings, and hung out with Elizabeth and Estheree on Friday nights when their boyfriends were not in town. I even taught Vacation Bible School. It was so much more refreshing as a teacher than as a student in the class.

GOLDEN NUGGET FOR GROWTH #10

It is one thing being a teenager with no responsibility and having someone else in charge of your life, but it's quite another when you must start making decisions for yourself. When you must not only face the handwriting on the wall, but also interpret it and act on what it means is when the true test starts. Teenagers think they have it so easy because they feel they do not have to make decisions and if they do, they can always change them. Once you are on your own, the steps you make are usually unretractable and you find yourself having to live with them for good or bad. But what is even worse is when you read and interpret that handwriting on the wall and you still don't know what to do with it. That can cause a real strain on the soul. Then is when you should realize that you need help. At such a time the best thing to do is relinquish all of it and give it to God.

God created us with a need for help. That need is not shameful nor is it a sign of failure. Scripture clearly lets us know that God wants us to acknowledge our needs. We see also throughout Scripture that God has created each of us with different strengths and has designed us to need help, and we honor Him when we ask for it. Asking for help is not admitting failure but recognizing that we do need God and he is there for us.

WHAT SCRIPTURE REVEALS ABOUT HOW TO ASK FOR HELP IN TIME OF NEED:

Psalm 46:1-3 (NIV)--"God is our refuge and strength, an ever-present help in trouble."

Proverbs 18:10 (KJV)--"The name of the Lord is a strong tower; the righteous run into it and are safe."

John 14:13-14 (KJV)--"Whatever you ask in my name, this I will do, that the Father may be glorified in the Son. If you ask me anything in my name, I will do it."

Psalm 121:2 (KJV)--"My help comes from the Lord, who made heaven and earth."

Matthew 7:7 (NIV)--"Ask, and it will be given to you; seek, and you will find; knock, and it will be opened to you."

John 15:16 (NIV)--"You did not choose me, but I chose you and appointed you that you should go and bear fruit and that your fruit should abide, so that whatever you ask the Father in my name, he may give it to you."

James 1:5 (NIV)--"If any of you lacks wisdom, let him ask God, who gives generously to all without reproach, and it will be given him."

Chapter 11: The Start of Real Love

Summer came and went, and I was still having a battle within ME. I went back to school in the fall and things were about the same. I landed a job in the science department as a research assistant to one of the biology professors. It was doing that year that I met Carl. One day I was gathering materials for Professor Blake's next day class, when a student came in. She was looking for Professor Blake. I told her he had gone for the day. She turned and started to leave and then stopped and turned around. I asked if there was anything I could help her with. She said, "I know you. Don't you remember me; you know, a couple summers ago in Delaware? I am Darlene Bagley. You worked at the drug store." Then I remembered, she was one of the teenagers I met the summer I stayed with my sister in Delaware and got a job at the store. I used to hang out with her and some of her friends. We talked for a while and later went to dinner at the dining hall together. She started coming by my room and hanging out with Estheree and me. We wondered why we had not run into each other our freshman year. I guess we were not in the right place at the right time.

We didn't go home for fall break and neither did she, but her brother, Carl, drove down from Delaware to bring her winter clothes. I just happened to be in her room when he came. She introduced us and, right away, there was something about him that

I just could not put my finger on. Later I asked her why I had never seen him that summer when I was in Delaware. She said that he was away in summer school that year. I also learned that he was now a senior history major at Cheyney State University in Pennsylvania. She said that when he graduated in the spring, he was going to graduate school for a master's in political science. He hoped to be a politician one day. (That should have been my cue to run like the wind, right then.) I just smiled and said, "He has his future all laid out, doesn't he?" She dropped down in a chair saying, "He has always been like that. When he knows what he wants he goes after it."

I just couldn't stop talking about him because he was so handsome. Estheree told me that I always see the extraordinary in the most ordinary people. But he was not just some ordinary person. That next weekend, Darlene told me that her brother wanted to know if it was OK to call me. I said yes and give her the number for the phone on our hall along with instructions about the best time to reach me. When she left, I wondered why I had done that and if that was a mistake. A looker like that must have a girlfriend. Estheree fell back on the bed and said, "You know why you gave her that number." That same night, I heard a knock at our door. It was one of the girls from down the hall. "Telephone, Bev." I was totally surprised when I picked up the phone and it was him. I could hear Isaac Hayes' "I Stand Accused" playing in the background. He said that he had wanted to call me since the day he was in his sister's dorm room. We talked about 30 minutes and I learned a lot about him; however, I was hesitant to share much about myself. I did learn that he lived off campus and he chose Cheyney University because it was a historically Black school and had been around since the 1830s. He also said that he had broken up with his girlfriend more than a year ago and he just had not had any desire to get serious about anybody else. He quickly added, "But now I have changed my mind."

I don't know if he had coached his sister to repeat exactly what he said, but she confirmed that he did break up with a girl more than a year ago about whom he had previously been very serious. He and I started communicating on a regular basis. He would send me 45 rpm records all the time with a note attached saying this is my plea to you. I remember several of those records very vividly: "When Somebody Loves You" by Teddy Pendergrass and "These Arms Are Mine" by Otis Redding. Estheree would say, "Girl, he is trying far too hard to get you."

He had a final exam scheduled on the day that we planned to leave school for Christmas break. Darlene went home on the train, so I didn't see him. During that break, he drove down to my home and you know my daddy gave him the third degree. Daddy did not like the fact that he was several years older than me. The day before New Year's Eve, he came back, and we went to New York to see a musical. That was his Christmas present to me. I couldn't believe that my parents were really letting me go with him, although I did almost have to request an act of Congress to get my daddy to say yes. I still believe the only reason that he relented was that we arranged for Estheree and her boyfriend to go, too. We had a wonderful time and spent the entire day looking around New York before the musical. We stayed at my sister's apartment that night and drove to his parents' house in Delaware the next day. They were just as nice as I had remembered them. They couldn't believe that we had gotten together. His father kept saying, "It was meant to be although it took a couple of years, but God does things in his own time," he said. I didn't say anything, but I already knew that. The warm feeling started welling up in my heart and I thought to myself, "Never postpone a chance for joy when you get it." On the third day, it was time to leave him and the three of us boarded the train for home. At the station, tears welled up in my eyes as Carl and I said goodbye. As the train pulled out from the station, I could see him still waving us goodbye and blowing kisses at me.

That is how my first real love started. After that, we got so close that we almost finished one another's sentences. The end of the year came, and Carl graduated. I worked at home that summer. Carl enrolled part time in graduate school at Delaware State, with intentions of teaching history at the high school in his hometown,

Wilmington, Delaware, that fall. We didn't see each other much that summer because his school schedule was very tight and, of course, I was working. My parents had planned a trip to Delaware to visit my sister for the Fourth of July week and I had a few days off to go with them. My sister said the first day, "I know why she's not cooking out with us this afternoon. She didn't really come to see us anyway, you know Carl lives here, too." Everybody had a good laugh.

In the fall of 1971, Carl did get the teaching position, and I went back to school to start my junior year, and life was good. Because of his studies and his teaching schedule, I didn't have the luxury of seeing him at school anymore. His sister Darlene had her own car and she drove herself back and forth now. Carl and I talked a lot on the phone, and I looked forward to getting together with him during fall break. When we weren't talking on the phone, I was writing him long letters and he was still sending me those love songs on 45 rpms with a note attached.

I had a heavier than usual schedule that semester and I had several projects pending. I just couldn't see how I would meet my deadlines if I went home. My mommy was really the one who made up my mind for me. One night I was talking to her on the phone and she said, "You must make some big girl decisions about this one. I know you want to come home and we want to see you, but how much are you going to get done if you come? You have to decide what you really need to do." Right then, I knew that I would be in the dorm over break. Estheree felt bad about leaving me but I knew she wanted to go home...for more reasons than one. I urged her to go on and to think nothing of it. After all, I was not the only person still on campus because a lot of people didn't go home during breaks.

I got my projects finished and was determined that when finals came around in December, I would breeze through them and be out of there on two wheels, going home. My parents were planning a big Christmas this year and all my sisters and their families would be there. When I got home, Carl and I talked on the phone and finally decided together that he would wait and come to see me the day after Christmas to give me time with my family. It was really his idea, not mine.

Christmas night after dinner, we were all gathered in the living room, Daddy at the piano, getting ready for our traditional Christmas singalong. When the telephone rang, nobody bothered to answer it at first. Then my younger brother picked it up and after a second or two said, "Fruitcake face (referring to me), you have a call from your dream boat." I jumped up and grabbed the phone from him, swatting the top of his head, "I told you about calling me names," I said. I walked the long phone cord into the next room and closed the door. When I said hello, I could hear Carl singing my favorite Christmas song by Darlene Love, "Christmas." He sung the entire song, every single word! By the time he had finished, I had slid down the wall and was sitting on the floor, with tears running down my face. His voice broke and I could hear that he was crying, too. I said, "Oh my goodness, I know you listen to a lot of love songs and send them to me, but I didn't know you could sing like that." We talked for a long time. I told him it was the best Christmas present ever. The last thing he said was that if it had not been snowing so hard, he would come tonight. Well, that was not exactly the last thing he said...Love is an amazing thing; love transforms things and love can make you see beyond walls.

When I opened the door, and put the phone back on the base, I noticed that daddy had moved from the piano and nobody was singing. They were just sitting there making small talk. My sister said, "You stayed on that phone long enough." I asked if they stopped singing because they were listening to our conversation. They just laughed. My oldest sister said, "It's OK, Bev, I know how you feel. I've been there, done that."

The family sat around late into the night talking about things that happened during our childhood like fights with Wesley James, the cucumber picking or lack of picking, the house filled with cousins and everything. Yes, a lot of thing have gone on at this house down this tree- lined path. When I finally crawled into bed, I thanked God for my wonderful family, my friends, and my newfound love, Carl.

When I got up the next morning, Mommy was already in the kitchen. Daddy was watching the news. He said that a lot of snow had fallen up North. He was telling Mommy that my sisters might have to postpone their trips home for a day or two. I went in the bathroom and closed the door and sat down on the side of the tub, wondering if that meant Carl couldn't get here today. Before I got the thought out of my head, the phone rang. It was Carl calling to tell me that he was snowed in. He wanted to take the train or the bus, but his father talked him out of that, saying that if the train could get through, he would spend most of his scheduled two-day visit traveling. As much as I wanted to see him, I agreed with his father. I didn't get to see Carl for Christmas because of the snow and my sisters didn't get to go home for two more days for the same reason. I was heartbroken because I had not really seen Carl since last year. I started to wonder how military wives handle staying away from their husbands for months at a time.

I managed to keep myself busy for the remainder of Christmas break. Shawn was home for the holidays also and on New Year's Eve, I rode with him, Elizabeth, Estheree, and her boyfriend to Watch Night Service. At midnight, after the benediction, we sat down in the back pew and made New Year's resolutions, secretly. The next week we all headed back to school.

Carl had made plans to take a long weekend to drive down to Clemson the second week in January to spend some time with me, after he got his students situated for the semester. I was very excited about that. Classes started and I reevaluated my spring semester schedule. I had registered for 18 hours, but now I was having second thoughts about the overload. Then I decided to switch out one of my electives for something easier. I looked down the schedule and saw Music: Piano 101. How I would love to play like my daddy, so without giving any more thought, I completed the drop/add slip and I was in music class. The first-class session was horrible. I played a lot worse than I sing, and you can't get any worse than that. At least learning to play would take my mind off things, though, and it did get better.

Carl came the second weekend and it was wonderful. We exchanged our belated Christmas gifts and we had fun going places around the city. He said that he always wanted to live in the South because of the mild weather, even in the wintertime. Winter has a way of messing up everything, especially our last Christmas, he said. We had a very pleasant weekend and both of us knew that our relationship was a lot more serious than we had realized. The last day in town, he wanted to take the three of us out to dinner (his sister Darlene, Estheree, and me). Both Darlene and Estheree said they would pass because he needed to spend that last day alone with me; after all, we had been robbed of Christmas together.

I cried when he got ready to leave and I believe he was crying behind those dark shades he put on just before he got in the car. We called each other almost every day; after that visit the 45 rpm records kept coming. One day he called me all excited because he had taken students from his History class to a debate match and they had won by a landslide. That conversation brought back memories of when I was on the debate team in high school. I told him that my high school team was unstoppable.

Everything that we said and every action during that telephone conversation that day made both of us realize that this was the start of real love.

GOLDEN NUGGET FOR GROWTH #11

I did then and I still believe that everything good that happens to me, God does it. Proverbs 11:25 (NIV) says, "A generous person will prosper; whoever refreshes others will be refreshed." This means that in living for the good of others, we shall be profited also ourselves. God has so constituted this universe, that selfishness is the greatest possible offense against His law, and living for others, caring and doing for others and, yes, loving others unselfishly is being obedient to His will. Our surest road to our own happiness is through seeking the happiness of our significant other. To get, we must give; to accumulate, we must scatter; to make ourselves happy, and become spiritually vigorous, we must do good, and seek the spiritual good of others.

All believers have some power to water others; some in ordinary ways, others in special ways. As we water others, we shall be watered ourselves. When in love, the watering becomes truly a special blessing. Loving each other, to me, is ministering to one another; ministering that includes love and compassion, a listening ear, prayers and blessings, as well as spiritual support. We are told in Scripture to enjoy our work, our mates, our children, our good health, our material blessings, and our God. Without the emotion of love, that would be impossible.

As a loving heart and helping hand is extended, joy is delivered to hearts.

WHAT SCRIPTURE SAYS ABOUT LOVING:

1 John 4:18 (ESV)--"There is no fear in love, but perfect love casts out fear. For fear has to do with punishment, and whoever fears has not been perfected in love."

Song of Solomon 3:4 (NIV)--"...I have found the one my heart loves."

John 15:12 (NIV)--"My command is this: Love each other as I have loved you."

I Corinthians 16:14 (NIV)--"Do everything in love."

Ephesians 5:21 (NIV)--"Submit to one another out of reverence for Christ."

1 John 4:8 (NIV)--"Whoever does not love does not know God, because God is love."

Ephesians 4:2 (NIV)--"Be completely humble and gentle; be patient, bearing with one another in love."

Chapter 12: Tragedy Strikes Twice

The day before spring break in 1972, Estheree's grandmother had a massive stroke. My daddy drove down to pick us up. We left in such a hurry that I forgot to pack my music to practice while at home. We didn't even go home, but instead Daddy drove straight to the hospital in the city, 35 miles away from our house. The doctors said that she probably wouldn't recognize anybody. At first, Daddy and I stayed in the waiting room with Estheree's grandfather and aunt so she could go in and have some time along with her grandmother. A little later I went on back to comfort her. When I walked in the ICU, her grandmother was gripping her hand and mouthing something I couldn't understand. But it was obvious that Estheree knew exactly what she was saying. The doctors couldn't believe how her condition had changed so quickly. We stayed at the hospital for hours but Estheree would not move when we got ready to leave. We prayed and then prepared to leave, taking her grandfather with us. Her aunt assured him that she would come later and bring Estheree with her.

Being the considerate people they were, my parents wouldn't let Estheree's grandfather go home alone. My mommy fixed him something to eat and insisted that he go in one of the bedrooms to rest and take a nap. Estheree and her aunt did not come that night. Early the next morning, her grandmother passed away. Daddy got her grandfather ready to take him back to the hospital. I insisted on going to be there for Estheree. Mommy patted me on my arm and told me to be strong for my friend. As she turned to go back into the house, she said, "Lord, I am glad we didn't let her grandfather go home by himself last night." Daddy stopped in town and picked up one of his friends to drive the aunt's car back, as he said he didn't think she should be driving.

When they got everything taken care of, we headed back, Daddy, Estheree, and me in one car, and her aunt, grandfather, and Daddy's friend in the other. Before we even got home, Mommy had started cooking food for the family and giving orders about how to pack everything to take over to Estheree's house. Arrangements were made and Estheree was a pillar of strength through that ordeal. We sat on the porch that night and she told me how much she loved her grandmother and that her grandparents and aunt and uncle were the only relatives she knew. Then the uncle died and left her aunt to take care of her grandparents. I knew her mother died when she was a baby and she never talked about her father, but I wasn't aware of all that she told me that night. We talked about the first time we met and how she stood up for me when we were in third grade. We hugged and reminded each other that we would be friends for life. When I got home later, Carl had called several times. To tell the truth, I had not had a chance to call him. I returned his call and he told me that

Darlene called and told him. He was as concerned about Estheree as I was.

The next day Elizabeth had gotten home on break as many of our other friends had. Together, we were a strong support system for Estheree. We were there for her in full force at the funeral. When spring break was over, everybody was concerned about her going back to school. She insisted that she was alright. My mommy and I rode out to her house because her aunt was really worried about her leaving so soon after the funeral. Mommy and Estheree went into the kitchen and shut the door. I don't know what they discussed, but when they came out my mommy hugged her aunt and said, "She's ready, let her go. You know that Bev will be there for her and if she should need to come back, you know George [my daddy] will go and get her for you."

We went back to school and both of us threw ourselves into our studies and I got good at playing the piano. My plan was to be able to play a love song for Carl by summer. Just as things were getting back to some form of normalcy, tragedy struck again. It was the week before final exams. I walked in the front door of the dorm and the assistant at the front desk told me I had an urgent message. She handed me the piece of paper and it said, "Urgent, please call Shawn immediately." There was a number to call under the note. I looked at it and thought, is he having a change of heart? I can't deal with him right now, Lord. Then I looked at the number again. That is my hometown prefix. What is he doing at home? Maybe he has flipped his lid. I picked up the phone and dialed the number. Shawn's mother answered the phone. When she realized it was me, she said, "I'm going to let you talk to Shawn. He's right here." Shawn came on the phone and without even saying hello, he just said, "Kirby." That was all he said, before he dropped the phone. I said hello about three times before he picked it up again. I could tell that he was crying. "My best friend, my best bud, Kirby is dead, Bev," he said. "What did you say, Shawn?" I asked. "Kirby was killed yesterday evening in a plane crash over Canada," he said. "Shawn, I need a minute, let me call you back," I said.

I guess I must have passed out, because the next thing I knew the dorm director, the assistant, and several other students were standing around me. One of the girls said, "I told the person on the phone not to worry, you would call him right back." Then my brain started to race, and I thought, "Lord, I can't do this by myself." The director told one of the girls to get my things and walk me to my room so I could lie down. I quickly said, "No, I need to go to Darlene Bagley's room." I just could not lay this on Estheree right now after all she just went through. I got to Darlene's room and told her one of my friends had been killed in a plane crash. I told her that I needed to call home.

The big sister on the hall had a phone in her room. Darlene walked down the hall with me, and I called Shawn back. He explained that Kirby's father was very sick, and Kirby got leave from his ship in the North Atlantic. He was hitching a ride home on a cargo plane when it crashed in bad weather, killing everybody on board. Shawn said he took the first plane home when his mother called and told him the news. I went back to Darlene's room until I could regain my composure, because the last thing I wanted to do was let Estheree see me like this so soon after her grandmother's death. Darlene insisted on calling Carl. I thought it not necessary, but I was glad to talk to him.

When I went to my room and told Estheree, she took it quite well. In fact, she was more concerned about me than I had been about her. Next thing she said was, "We have to get home." I talked to my mommy and she made a lot of sense, telling me that there was nothing I could do at home but grieve. Final exams are in a week and that I needed to first calm down, get some rest, and try to prepare for my finals. Once the arrangements were made, Daddy would come and get me for the funeral, she said. I knew what she was saying made the most sense.

The funeral was scheduled for that Saturday. Estheree and I made arrangements through the academic dean for taking our final exams late and my daddy picked us up that Friday afternoon.

That night, we went over to Kirby's house. His father was home from the hospital, but I could tell that he probably should have been back in a hospital bed, but he had insisted on coming home. The whole gang was at the wake when we got to the church, and it was that night that we planned our surprise tribute for the funeral. We talked to Kirby's mother and she said it was OK. We told nobody else and it wasn't even on the order of service.

Kirby's brother said that he was going to drive the pink Pontiac in the funeral procession and wanted some of us to ride with him. After the wake, we stayed at church to practice. Next day, six of us rode in Kirby's car, behind the family car; the other six in a car right behind it, just like old times, except Kirby wasn't with us.

When it was time, during the service, Pastor Reid got up and said, "Now, Kirby's closest friends will pay tribute to the family in memory of Kirby." I had not thought of it before, but I wondered if Kirby's father would be alright through this. He had been wheeled in a reclining wheelchair and had a nurse on each side. The funeral attendants opened the casket with Kirby lying there in his service dress uniform of a naval officer. He was so handsome and manly. I had to bite my lip to keep from crying. We all got up at the same time. I walked over to the piano and took my seat and the whole church got quiet. My fingers started moving across that keyboard and the group opened with "I'm Free, Praise the Lord, I'm Free...."

The place became a wall of calm. I must admit they were brave and strong because not one of them cried through the entire song. Of course, I can't say that for myself. Tears were steaming down my face by the time I played the last note. I could hear myself yelling, "Yes, Lord; yes, Lord; he's free."

At the repast, everybody wanted to know when I had learned to play the piano. My parents knew I was taking a piano class but had no idea I could play that well. Before the meal was over, Kirby's father had to be rushed back to the hospital. That night, when we finally got home, my dad said he believed I had been holding back on him all those years. My brother asked, "Did you learn how to sing, too, while you were learning the piano?" I jokingly said, "God does perform miracles but let's not get carried away here."

I went back to school the following Monday morning, took my finals, and that was the end of my junior year. What a taxing year for all of us. I thought about all that had happened in just a matter of months. Then the poem "Footprints in the Sand" came to mind and I said, "This semester, Lord, I know you carried me."

GOLDEN NUGGET FOR GROWTH #12

During our lifetime, we all see pain, joy, hope, and fear and we on occasions grieve, but also, as we go through those emotions, they in some way give a comforting sense of God's presence in our lives. When we lose a loved one, it may feel as if a part of ourselves has been taken with them. We grieve because we no longer have an opportunity to share with them or realize our dreams with them. Though this pain is real and deep, if our loved ones belong to Jesus, we can take comfort, with certainty, that one day we will see them again.

God doesn't want us to live in fear of death, but to live well and die knowing that we belong to a risen Savior who has already defeated death for us. As Philippians 1:21 (NIV) says, "For me, to live is Christ and to die is gain." This simply means that life on this earth is meant to live for the Lord, but death will be even better because we will then be in the presence of the Lord.

No matter how we feel about death, we can rest assured that it is not the end and we can overcome it if we just believe. Normal people do grieve, but that does not mean that they must fear death, nor do they have to die alone. Scripture tells us that death primarily means separation—separation of man's spirit from his body and of man from God. Our souls, however, are eternal. Jesus will return one day; this should give us hope and peace as we endure all the chaos in this broken world.

Thanks be to God! He gives us victory through our Lord, Jesus Christ"

WHAT SCRIPTURE SAYS ABOUT DEATH:

Romans 14:8 (NIV)--"If we live, we live for the Lord; and if we die, we die for the Lord. So, whether we live or die, we belong to the Lord."

Romans 8:13 (NIV)--"For if you live according to the flesh, you will die; but if by the Spirit you put to death the misdeeds of the body, you will live."

Ecclesiastes 12:7 (NIV)--"And the dust returns to the ground it came from, and the spirit returns to God who gave it."

John 3:16 (NIV)--"For God so loved the world that he gave his one and only Son, that whoever believes in him shall not perish but have eternal life."

Ezekiel 18:32 (NIV)--"For I take no pleasure in the death of anyone, declares the Sovereign Lord. Repent and live!"

Chapter 13: Oaths and Vows: Marriage on the Horizon

As I approached the last summer of my college years, I started making plans for my life. I would be a senior when I returned to Clemson in the fall and I wanted to be fully prepared. I sought assistance from the head of the Biology Department, and he helped me get my feet wet again at the biomedical research company in Durham, North Carolina. I jumped at the chance because the pay was very good for a college student. My mommy and I drove up one weekend and I rented a room in a boarding house near Research Triangle Park, in nearby Chapel Hill, North Carolina.

My tight T-Twelve gang had started to grow apart and were thinking about making their own mark in the world. Estheree's boyfriend chose to go to summer school, getting in extra hours so he could graduate on time the next spring. She went to Virginia and got a job working in the personnel office at a major tobacco company because that was a chance to be near him. Plus, it was a lucrative cigarette company and the salaries there were the best in Richmond.

The work at the research facility was not hard, but very intense. However, I had lot of time in the evening and on weekends to relax. Usually, I would hang around the boarding house in the evenings and talk to the owners, who were an older couple in their

70s. They also had one other boarder, a young lady from England who was a student at one of the nearby universities. She wasn't around very much...spent most of her time on campus in the library. However, living there was almost like being at home because the couple had mannerisms exactly like my parents.

On Sunday mornings they would invite the other boarder and me to church with them. She would go sometimes, but I would always go. One night I went downstairs, and they were watching television in their private living room. They naturally said to come on in. I had never been in that part of the house. In the front of the room facing the big picture window was the most beautiful baby grand piano I had ever seen. I walked over and rubbed my palm over the shiny black cover and asked, "Who plays?" They both spoke at the same time, "We both do." They told me that is the way they met and the reason they were married to this very day. They went on to talk about how the two of them dreamed of becoming concert pianists, but because of the times before integration, they were not allowed in most establishments and concert halls to perform where they would get the opportunity. They eventually gave up that dream and settled on each other. They took an oath to always work to make things better for others than they had for themselves. They also vowed to purchase a concert-style piano of their very own when they were able. They kept the oath and worked vigorously during the Civil Rights Era for equal rights for everybody and, of course, they keep the vow because the piano was sitting right there in their home. However, that was not the only oath and vow that I would talk about that summer.

I admired that piano and asked if they would play something for me because I loved music and had just recently started playing myself. Instead of playing for me, they asked me to play something for them, and I did. They were amazed and said the piece I played was most beautiful. "What else can you play?" They asked. I rattled off a few of my most favorites. That Sunday when we went to church, the minister of music came over and told me that he heard that I enjoyed playing and would like for me to play the closing hymn at the end of the service. I assured him that I only played a little and couldn't take on such a huge task without practicing. I looked back on the second pew and both of my landlords were waving and nodding their heads, yes. I had very little choice but to agree. When the time came, the pastor announced me, and I sat down and played as the choir bellowed out the most beautiful renditions of "Amazing Grace." After that, they would always invite me to choir practice to play but I didn't take them up on it because I knew I couldn't sing.

The next weekend I decided to go home. That Saturday afternoon, I sat on the front porch admiring the row of trees that lined the path to the highway. I started reminiscing about my high school days. I decided to go visit Kirby's father, who had been in a nursing home since Kirby's death. When he left the hospital after the funeral, he was never able to go home again. I slipped out of my shorts and pulled on a cool sundress. As I took the car keys from the hook beside the kitchen door, I called back and told my mommy that I was taking the car into town for a while.

When I got to the nursing home, Kirby's mother was just leaving. After making small talk with her, I went in. There was a picture on the windowsill and his father was propped up in a chair near the window. He started to smile and with his limited movement, he reached out his hand to me. I caught his hand and he gave me a handshake with a much firmer grip than I thought he was capable of. He said, "This is a pleasant surprise to get a visit from a pretty girl on a hot Saturday afternoon." I smiled and as he released my hand, I could see Kirby all over his face; in fact, he looked like an older vision of Kirby. We talked for a while and he shared how he missed working in his garage. After a while, he looked straight ahead and said, "Tell you something else I miss, too. My boy...I really do miss him." I touched his arm and replied, me too, me too. He went on saying, "You know, if my boy had lived, you would be in that picture with him because he was going to marry you and he would have gotten a good catch, too." But he said, "He died doing one of the things that was really important to him. He always dreamed of being an officer in the U.S. Navy.

After leaving the nursing home, I drove out to Perkin's Pond. I just sat in the car and let my mind go back to the last time I saw him. Kirby was the best friend I had other than Estheree. We were closer than Shawn. Kirby and I loved each other, but were not romantically in love, because we realized that "being in love" would mess up what we had; the best friendship in the world. I vowed that afternoon that I would never let his memory die and, no matter what, a part of his spirit will always be in my heart.

The next couple of weeks were especially rough. I talked to Carl almost every night, but I was still lonesome. I just felt like I needed to see him. One Thursday evening when I left work, he called. He said he could feel something strange in my voice. I confessed that I really missed him. He suggested that I hop on the train the next day after work and come on up and he would drive me back on Sunday. The only thing, I had committed to going to Richmond that weekend to hang out with Estheree. "OK," Carl said, "I will meet you there. When your train gets there, I will be there." So, I went!

We had a wonderful time and it was good to see Estheree. This time with Carl was much different than usual. I couldn't put my finger on it, but I knew it was special. That Saturday night we were sitting on the couch in Estheree's apartment and he asked me if I had heard the new song by Al Wilson, called "Show and Tell." Before I could answer, he started bellowing out the lyrics..."These are the eyes that never knew how to smile, till you came into my life...And these are the arms that long to lock you inside, every day and every night." He dropped down on one knee and said, "Right here, right now, I take an oath to love you for the rest of my life. Will you marry me?" With that said, he pulled out a little black velvet box, opened it, and took out the most beautiful ring I had ever seen. I said yes right away. He told me that he had purchased the ring at the end of the school year but was waiting until the end of summer when I went home so he could properly ask my parents for my hand in marriage. However, he made up his mind when he talked to me on Thursday that he couldn't wait.

We called my parents and then we called his. All of them were so thrilled and wanted to know when we had planned the wedding. That was just it, we hadn't planned to be engaged, let along planned a wedding. We, however, made a lot of plans on the drive back to Chapel Hill. When we got to the boarding house, it felt good to introduce him as my fiancé. My landlords said, "Well, you left for the weekend going for milk and you came back with the whole cow." We just laughed. In honor of our engagement, they played a few jazz numbers on their baby grand piano. Carl also sang a few tunes as they played. I listened! We had a late dinner and by the time Carl was ready to get on the road, he was exhausted. Acting like the parents we didn't have there, they insisted that he not try to drive back to Delaware that night and suggested a nice motel in Chapel Hill. So, he stayed. Before he left for the motel, he told me to get up early and he would pick me up for breakfast before I went to work. When he dropped me off at the research plant after breakfast, I didn't want to see him go. He assured me that we would see each other again real soon. Watching him drive off was one of the hardest things I had ever done.

I went through work that day in slow motion. The weeks ahead seemed to just crawl along and talking to him every night always turned into a crying party. One thing that really warmed my heart was the day I came home from work and there was a package on the hall table for me. It was a stack of 45 rpm love songs. Attached to each of the records was an explanation for why he had chosen each one. In the letter included in the package with the records, he told me that when I got lonely to just play the records and pretend that he was talking to me. I played them every night.

Finally, summer came to an end and I was ready to go home. On my last day at work, my supervisor told me that the VP of clinical research wanted to see me. When I walked into that plush office on the third floor, I didn't know what to expect. He motioned for me to have a seat. He said, "Ms. Martin, I have heard some wonderful things about you and your work ethics, and I understand that you will be graduating next spring. I also understand that you plan to go on to graduate school studying health policy administration. You know we have some of the best graduate schools here in the area. What do you say about a permanent position here with us?" I was taken by surprise, but I didn't hesitate to say," Yes, I would love to work here," I said. "OK, it's settled then," he said. "When you get ready to graduate in the spring, get in touch with our personnel office and we will bring you down and get you squared away."

My daddy picked me up a few days later. It seemed like I had 10 years' worth of things in that room at the boarding house. I thanked my landlords for making me feel right at home all summer and promised to invite them to the wedding. I also asked them to be a part of my program of wedding music at the ceremony. After all, it's not every day you get real celebrities to play at your wedding, I smiled.

GOLDEN NUGGET FOR GROWTH #13

People tend to make commitments every day. Whether it be a vow, an oath, or a simple promise, it is intended to be and should be binding. Because making a commitment involves dedicating ones' self to something, some person, or some platform, t also becomes an obligation. Some commitments are large, like marriage, which is a vow intended for life. Agreeing to take a job is a commitment to show up and do the work and a promise is made for you to get paid for doing the work. Committed individuals have a balance between what they want with what they're capable of doing. If you have a commitment to yourself, you will more likely be committed to other people and other things.

Those who believes in God and confess that Jesus Christ lived, died, and rose on the third day to save man from sin have faith. If they have faith it will be evident in their attitude and their behavior because they are spiritually committed. When they are spiritually committed, they are not going to take lightly the oaths, vows, and promises they make, because to break them would be sinning.

God has entrusted something valuable to each believer to be proclaimed through faith. As God is committed to every believer, they in turn are responsible for being committed to others and to serve others. We are not exercising faithfulness to God if we cannot keep our commitment to our fellow man.

Oaths, vows, and promises should be binding, forever. When you lose focus on your commitments, go to Matthew 6:33 (NIV), which says, "But seek first His kingdom and His righteousness, and all these things will be given to you as well."

WHAT SCRIPTURE SAYS ABOUT COMMITMENT AND JESUS'
PROMISE:

Psalm 37:5 (KJV)--"Commit your way to the LORD, trust also in
Him, and He shall bring it to pass."

2 Corinthians 5:19 (KJV)--"That God was in Christ reconciling the
world to Himself, not imputing their trespasses to them, and has
committed to us the word of reconciliation."

Psalm 31:5 (KJV)--"Into Thine hand I commit my spirit; Thy hast
redeemed me, O Lord God of truth."

Job 5:8 (NKJV)--"But as for me, I would seek God, and to God I
would commit my cause."

Proverbs 16:3 (KJV)--"Commit your works to the Lord, and your
thoughts will be established."

Romans 8:28 (NIV)--"And we know that in all things God works for
the good of those who love him, who have been called according
to his purpose."

Chapter 14: Preparation for a Lifetime of Love

With the start of my senior year at Clemson came a new me. I became more laid back and less anxious about everything. I studied, perfected my piano skills, and made plans for my wedding. We had decided on a date the next summer, July 24, 1973, as our wedding day because it fell on a Saturday, my birthday. We felt that late July would give me a chance to catch my breath and unwind enough to be a prepared bride, after graduation. Carl was still teaching at the high school in Delaware, but he was also pursuing other interests as well. He was a real politician at heart and was vying for an important position with the city of Wilmington. Delaware seemed like a likely starting point for him, but he really wanted to be a senator in Washington, D.C.

One night I was talking to Carl on the phone and this tingling sensation came over me. The sensation that always made me know that God had me; that I was covered. I guess that is what made me ask him the serious question of whether this would be forever. First, he said he didn't understand the question and after a minute or two, he asked me why I asked such a question. The first thing that came to his mind was that I was having second thoughts about getting married. I assured him that I had a reason for asking. I had seen people fall in and out of love before and wondered if they had given any thought to the fact that they made vows for a lifetime. My parents have been married for many, many years and they are happy. In my heart I don't think they ever get tired of being with each other, although they do have disagreements sometimes. However, I do know almost with certainty that they would not choose anybody else with whom to spend the rest of their lives. I cannot exactly say that about my sisters yet because they haven't been married for a long, long time, although I believe they love their husbands. But I do look at some married couples and see how miserable their lives are and wonder why they ever got married in the first place. Some of them treat each other poorly, some of them cheat, and some of them just stay together for convenience and/or perhaps for security...they think they are better off together than apart. So, I guess what I am asking you, I said to Carl, is, "Are you willing to go into this for the long haul, until death do us part and to work hard at marriage, no matter what, to make love be the cement that will always keep our marriage together?" His answer was, "I totally and truly love you and I am prepared to live with, love, and cherish you until I die. Furthermore, I will never do anything to cause mistrust, or unhappiness to you, intentionally. Besides, if you don't know me by now, you will never ever know me, because all that we have been through should give you the answer." I laughed and said, "I recognize those last words. You are saying the words to one of your songs, aren't you?" He just laughed.

We changed the subject and he told me that the position as city manager with the city of Wilmington looked very favorable for him and he would take it, if the opportunity arose. I was happy for him because it was amazing for a young man not yet 25, a man of color to land that job, during those times.

Fall break came and went and Christmas was coming up. Carl got the job as city manager for the city of Wilmington, effective January 30. That was perfect timing. The semester would have just ended, and he could resign from the high school where he was teaching with a seamless transition. His parents had a small celebration for him over the Christmas holidays and my parents and I drove up to celebrate with him.

When I got back to school in January, the wedding was on. I had so much to do and I was forever busy. I tried to spread everything out so it would not pile up all at once. Just before final exams, Darlene and Estheree got together with some of our friends at school and had a bridal shower for me. It was wonderful and I don't know until this day how they kept it a secret from me until that very day. A few days after the shower I contacted Human Resources at the company in Durham and arranged a meeting. I was extremely thankful when finals were over. I took a trip to Durham, met someone from Human Resources and the vice president of clinical research. I was not only offered a job, but also a very generous sign-on bonus, with a start date of August 1. As I hit the interstate in the rental car, heading back to school, I thought to myself…never would I have thought that I could land such a position at such a prestigious company, a Black girl, in the '70s, fresh out of college. God is good!

I graduated summa cum laude, at the top of my class. I received all types of honors and accolades. Estheree and Darlene didn't do so badly themselves. My family, Carl and his parents, Estheree's boyfriend, and aunt were all there to celebrate with us. When I got home, my parents and sisters had bought me a little chocolate brown Pinto as a graduation present, my very first car. After a few days of doing nothing, I got busy finalizing plans for my wedding, work, and for graduate school. Everybody kept saying, "That is a bit much for you to undertake in one summer." Actually, there wasn't that much to do, because my mommy and sisters had taken care of most of the things for the wedding, under my directions from school, of course.

The first week in June, I drove up to Durham and met Carl at the airport so we could look for a place for me to live. We found a spacious apartment in downtown Durham, large enough for both of us because he would be spending a lot of time there also, after we get married in July. It was a bit pricy, but I could afford it with my new salary and Carl's new position back in Delaware.

What makes one fall in love? What inspires two people to get married? What makes two people fall in love and what inspires two people to get married, in my opinion, are two different things. Where there is love there is life. When a couple falls in love, they feel each other's joy, pain, and heartache. They feel there is nothing more important, aside from God, than each other. They feel like they can stay locked in a cubicle forever without food or water, and still survive on each other's love. On the other hand, the inspiration to get married may be for love, appearance, or because that is the thing to do. In some cases, love has nothing to do with it. As I see it, God intended for a man and a woman to be inspired by the Holy Spirit to love each other unconditionally and prepare to become as one flesh before they take the marriage step.

To me, there are three things that are most critical prerequisites for marriage, I think. Both people should be honest about knowing themselves, as well as knowing each other holistically, know what forgiveness looks like, and have trust so strong between the two of them that no outsider can break. That bond will hold them together. That is why marriage should not be rushed. A couple should take some time to watch, examine the mannerisms and actions of their partner in different situations, before that step is taken. However, not all couples have to be compatible to get married, if they have love in their heart, have compassion, and understand the attributes of each other. Because if they have love in their hearts, they know God, and He will guide their actions.

An ideal marriage is one where there is love but there is also serenity. There must be a certain amount of tranquility, calm, and peacefulness, and there is as much respect as there is love. The biggest need aside from love is togetherness. As partners, they must be together on the path they take in everything.

A "perfect couple" is a happy couple who enjoys time together, values each other, and maintains a strong bond. "No couple is truly 'perfect,' but you and your partner can become your own version of a perfect couple. Start by building trust and developing healthy communication habits. Additionally, spend quality time together to strengthen your bond" (Dr. William Gardner, Psy.D.).

Learning to live and love through the lens of faith will give you a new perspective for your marriage. Proverbs 24:27 (NIV) says, "Put your work in order and get your fields ready; after that, build your house." In a spiritual sense, the heart must be first cleared of thorns, opened to genial influences, before the man can build up the fabric of virtuous habits, and thus arrive at the virtuous character before you say, "I do."

WHAT SCRIPTURE SAYS ABOUT PREPARING FOR MARRIAGE:

Hebrews 13:4 (ESV)--"Let marriage be held in honor among all, and let the marriage bed be undefiled, for God will judge the sexually immoral and adulterous."

1 Corinthians 13:4-7 (ESV)--"Love is patient and kind; love does not envy or boast; it is not arrogant or rude. It does not insist on its own way; it is not irritable or resentful; it does not rejoice at wrongdoing but rejoices with the truth. Love bears all things, believes all things, hopes all things, endures all things."

Genesis 2:18 (ESV) --"Then the Lord God said, "It is not good that the man should be alone; I will make him a helper fit for him.""

Genesis 2:24 (ESV)--"Therefore a man shall leave his father and his mother and hold fast to his wife, and they shall become one flesh."

Proverbs 3:5-6 (KJV)--"Trust in the Lord with all your heart and lean not on your own understanding; in all your ways acknowledge Him, and He shall direct your paths."

Chapter 15: Ten Years of Wedded Bliss

A couple of days before the wedding, my house was like Grand Central Station. We had my younger brother running errand, and my younger sisters trying on lacy dresses and such. The girls were loving it, but my brother threatened to jump in my Pinto and drive far, far away until the chaos was over. Then everybody started coming in for the wedding. My sister from New York, my cousin Dorthea and her father were at our house, my sister and family from Delaware were at my sister's house in town. We put Carl, his parents, and other relatives and friends in a motel in the city, 35 miles away.

The night before the wedding we had our rehearsal and afterward, dinner in the church fellowship hall. We wanted the meal catered; my mommy, on the other hand, wouldn't hear of it and prepared a meal fit for a king, with the help of some of the ladies from the church's women's auxiliary. With immediate family, friends, and the bridal party, we fed more than 70 people at the rehearsal dinner.

Estheree, Elizabeth, Darlene, and two other young ladies from T-Twelve were bridesmaids, my sister who lived in New York was the maid of honor, and my two younger sisters were junior bridesmaids. My niece and nephew were the flower girl and the ring bearer, respectively. Three of Carl's friend from Delaware, my cousin Willie, and my two brothers-in-law were groomsmen, and Shawn and Estheree's boyfriend were ushers.

The reception was held at the First Baptist Church annex in town because it was twice as large as our church fellowship hall, and we had 200-plus people in attendance. The wedding was beautiful, and my father was so handsome as he walked me down the aisle. Yes, the wedding was beautiful, but the reception was just marvelous. I kept my word and the couple who owned the boarding house in Chapel Hill performed the most breathtaking program of music. As a surprise for Carl, I played the piano and Elizabeth sang "When God Made You." She had been the best singer in our high school glee club, and she nailed that song. Carl had the same idea, because he surprised me by singing "Flesh of My Flesh." I will never forget that wonderful day. We had planned a honeymoon in the Bahamas, but because I had committed to start work on August 1, we put that on hold until the Christmas break. We went to the Eastern Shore Maryland for four days and then came back to Durham to set up the apartment.

I went to work in August and enrolled in graduate school at the University of North Carolina at Chapel Hill, taking two classes in the evening. It was not easy living apart from my husband, but we had already discussed that we would make the sacrifice for a while. Prayer and my Comforter were the glue that kept me together and kept me going. Carl would take a commuter flight down almost every Friday evening for the weekend and I would take the train to Delaware when I could get a Friday and Monday off together. That lasted for a year, at which time my company merged with another company and opened additional corporate offices in Philadelphia. At that time, I transferred to that office that was about a 40-minute drive from Wilmington via the interstate. I enrolled in graduate studies at the University of Delaware. Carl was a very successful city manager and was being groomed for a bid for the Delaware State Senate. He was eager and I was excited for him because that was his dream to become a politician.

We bought a house in suburban Wilmington and life was good. Carl ran for a seat in the senate but lost. He was a little disappointed at first. Then one Sunday we were at church and the pastor preached this profound sermon about trusting God and not giving up. "Whatever you do, work at it with all your heart, as working for the Lord, not for human masters" Colossians 3:23 (NIV). After the service, I was standing on the sidewalk waiting for Carl to bring the car around from the parking lot when I got this strange feeling that Carl would be alright. When he pulled up to the curb and I opened the door to get in he said, "Beverly Marie Martin Bagley, I am going to run for a senate seat again, and I have faith that I will win." I just smiled, patted his arm, and said, "I believe you will." The next week, we found that I was pregnant with our first child. At the end of that semester, I put my graduate studies on hold.

By the time I took maternity leave, everybody thought for sure that I would pop. I had a beautiful baby boy, Christopher, 9 pounds and 10½ ounces. He was my husband's pride and joy. Carl was wrapped up in family and work and decided not to plan for a bid for a Senate seat next term. When my son was 4 years old, I had my second child, Carla. It was at that time that I took a leave of absence from work. Carl got a promotion and with an assistant, it made it easier for him to be home at regular hours every day.

When Christopher started school, we put Carla in day care, and I went back to work. Carl's mother was a godsend. She would pick the kids up in the afternoon and bring them home about the time I got there. Most days she timed it just right, pulling into the driveway about the time I did. Sometimes her husband would be with her and a complete fixed dinner was in the trunk and they would spend the night, so Carl and I could have some "us" time, as they called it. We tried to protest, but they insisted that they loved spending time with the grands. "After all, we are retired now, and we are free to do whatever we desire to do," they said.

Carl did run for the senate again and won. With that he spent a lot of time in Dover at the legislature. He had served two terms in the Senate when Carla turned 5 years old and we had our third child, Clarissa.

When Clarissa was still a toddler, I became ill. I thought I was just tired because I had a lot on my plate and Carl was gearing up for a United States Senate run. He had tough competition and it took a lot to prepare; however, he was concerned and thought that he should drop out of the race. I insisted that he press on, brushing it off as I just needed a little rest. One day, I got so sick that I had to pull over on the interstate coming home from work. A highway patrolman stopped to assist and called for emergency transport. I was taken to the hospital and after a couple days of tests, was diagnosed with pancreatic cancer. Carl had me transferred to the best hospital around in Baltimore. I had surgery and started treatments. My parents came to help assist us because Carl was dividing his time between taking care of me, work, and the campaign.

After several months I was doing better but had to go back into the hospital for routine tests. The night before I was due to be discharged, Carl called instead of coming back to the hospital. He told me he thought his parents needed a break and he had gotten the kids to bed and would be there early the next morning to pick me up. I thought nothing of it at the time. Next day he picked me up, took me home, and went to run necessary errands. Before he returned, his mother came in with the children from school, as usual. I learned that she had the children at her house the night before. When Carl returned, I was waiting for him to clarify, but he did not. That night he sat downstairs in his office until very late. When he came to bed, it was obvious that he had been crying. The only thing he said was, "I just want to hold you in my arms." I felt really sorry for him, knowing what he must be going through.

Next morning, he got the children ready, took them to school and day care and returned, telling me he decided not to go in to work that day. When I came downstairs, he was fixing breakfast. I sat at the table while he finished. Suddenly, he fell right at my knee and started singing Otis Redding's "These Arms of Mine" like the old days. I could feel the tears falling down my face onto his head as he sang and my heart was breaking for him, until he said, "I broke my vows." I went stiff. He explained that it happened on Sunday afternoon. Knowing he could not face me, he said he decided not to come back to the hospital. He told me he was at the office with one of the campaign workers who was helping him review some campaign material. He was so worried about me, and drained. She started to cry because she and her friend were having problems. She was asking his advice when she fell apart; he was consoling her, and it just happened.

I must have lost it because I shoved him away and just kept shouting, "How could you?" He was just sitting there on the kitchen floor looking up at me as if he didn't recognize the person that had emerged. I went into the den and buried my face in the arm of my favorite chair. He came in and begged me to forgive him and promised that it would never happen again. "It was a mistake, I put down my guard and it should not have happened," he said. I looked up and said, "We cannot go on as if nothing has happened. I have to leave." Everything after that became fuzzy, but I know that he went on begging for more than an hour. I remembered him asking me if I would be alright or if I wanted some time alone. I simply said, "Get out!"

With silence in the room I sat up and the poem "Footprints in the Sand" came to mind. I thought there must be only one set in the sand now because I felt sure the Lord was carrying me. My worn Bible was on the table beside my chair. I picked it up and it automatically opened to the 23rd Psalm. I read it out loud.

Shortly, the phone rang, and I did not answer it. After it kept ringing, I decided to answer. It was my sister. The only thing she said was "I just talked to Carl and I will be over in a few minutes." When she arrived after she held me and we cried together, she told me that Carl had come to her job and told her everything and asked her to come, not that he had to ask. He said that he had no one else to go to. A little later, Carl's mother and father arrived. His mother burst into the den sobbing profusely, asking, "Lord, what has my son done, why did he do such a thing?" She came to me and hugged me tight, telling me she wished she knew how to fix this. The four of us stood there embracing each other. Nobody could understand how this could happen after we had spent more than 10 years in a loving marriage.

While trying to explain several days later, Carl inadvertently alluded that the only reason he told me about the incident was because he thought someone had seen them. Things went from bad to worse and I got to the point that I did not want to be in the same house with him. He unwillingly moved out, but was back every single day, explaining and begging for forgiveness. In all my 30-something years, I had never hated anybody, not even my third-grade teacher, but I wanted to hate him. I felt that if I could just hate him, I could move forward, but I couldn't. The Lord kept quietly telling me, "You are better than that; just put your trust in me."

After coming every day for weeks, being with the children, and trying to do everything for me (and I wouldn't let him), we took another step. I knew it was time to turn the page. It was so odd, one day I woke up and I just could not get Romans 12:19 (NIV) out of my head, "Do not take revenge, but leave room for God's wrath: for it is written, It is mine to avenge; I will repay," says the Lord.

When Carl came over that evening, he played with the children, he helped with their homework, and put them to bed. I was in the den when he came downstairs. He wanted to talk (more like beg) again. I knew it was time. I listened to him plead his case for the millionth time and explain how he thinks she set him up and how it will never happen again. When he finished, it was my turn. I told him that I had forgiven him, but I don't think it will ever be possible for me to forget. Then I asked him if he remembered many years ago before we got married, I asked him a question, "Do you want to get married for a reason or for a season?" He slowly said, yes. "Well," I said, "You have proven to me that you got married for a season because I cannot see how you could do what you did and still think our marriage is alright." I told him that I looked at our marriage as a covenant, a relationship based on promises and commitment, not just feelings—I told him that I married him for a reason, and I never ever thought of doing anything to hurt our marriage even under insurmountable pressure because love is most certainly an important piece of a marriage. It was at that point that I told him that I loved him very much and probably always would, but I wanted a divorce.

In a few days, he ended his bid for the U.S. Senate seat and threw himself into his work and his children. He also kind of distanced himself from his parents. He never stopped trying to get back with me right up to the day the divorce papers were signed. Even now, he will laughingly say to me, "Bev, I thought you were eventually going to let me come back home, but you never did."

In my marriage, we lived well, laughed often, and loved much. Our marriage was one great joy after another and one big bump caused it to end. When it got to the point that I felt I had given all that I could give, I decided that was enough. I threw out all possibilities of compromise. I do not know if I made the right choice. It was instilled in me to forgive and I did that, but I just could not go on as if nothing had happened. There is no doubt about it, though, I loved my husband with all my heart; I loved him more than anyone will ever know. I guess I will love him until I die, for it is said, the first love is the only real love. The day he walked into that dorm room at Clemson University, I knew he was my chosen one. The trouble is, I was not willing to compromise or share him with another woman.

GOLDEN NUGGET FOR GROWTH #15

There are two hurtful situations that occur between a married couple who love each other: a wound and a wrong. The wound does not require forgiveness because it is usually unintentional and accidental, so time and patience will take care of it. The other situation, though, is a different story. A wrong is when a person knows that what he is doing will hurt the other person and does it anyway. It is a moral dilemma. To wrong someone you love requires forgiveness. Forgiveness, though, does not come easy, once it is done it's done, even if it is not forgotten, but trust must be built back over time. Forgiveness takes care of the damage done. However, the true test of love will be how the person works to rebuild that trusting relationship and sometimes that never comes.

If I were to use just two words to describe the ideal marriage, I would choose dedication and effort. Dedication means that you work so hard that nothing else can possibly derail it and you must put forth effort every minute of every day to make sure it does not derail. There are other terms that help to make an ideal marriage, like compromise, Christ-filled, and respect, but I think unless you are dedicated to putting forth every effort, you might derail when the tracks ahead become warn or damaged.

Usually when a marriage is about to fail, you know because there are warning signs. The signs generally are evident over time. There's a little piece shattered here and a broken piece there. With my marriage, I didn't see it coming; it just happened and the whole thing shattered into a million pieces all at once. I suppose that is why it was so difficult to pick up the pieces and move on.

In our 10 years of marriage, I never felt drained and he never gave any indication that the marriage was draining him. We both were very reliable, trustworthy partners. Our private thoughts were open books to each other, and shared intimacy was important in our relationship. We apologized when we made mistakes and shared things with each other that no one else ever knew. We did mess up sometimes, and we said we were sorry and forgave. But some mistakes are too big to just forget and move on.

There are many ways to deal with a cheating spouse. But before you deal directly with him and his cheating, you need to take care of you and figure out what you want from this, whether the relationship is reconcilable or if you need to leave. Whatever you decide will be for keeps, so you better well get it right the first time and know that you will have to rely heavily on Philippians 4:13 (NIV): "I can do all this through Christ who gives me strengthens."

WHAT SCRIPTURE HAS TO SAY ABOUT FORGIVENESS, INFIDALITY, AND DIVORCE:

Proverbs 6:32 (NIV)--"But a man who commits adultery has no sense; whoever does so destroys himself."

Luke 6:27-28 (NIV)--"Love your enemies, do good to those who hate you, bless those who curse you, pray for those who mistreat you."

Corinthians 6:18 (NIV)--"Flee from sexual immorality. All other sins a person commits are outside the body, but whoever sins sexually, sins against their own body."

Exodus 20:14 (NIV)--"You shall not commit adultery."

Hebrews 13:4 (NIV)--"Marriage should be honored by all, and the marriage bed kept pure, for God will judge the adulterer and all the sexually immoral."

Matthew 19:9 (NIV)--"I tell you that anyone who divorces his wife, except for sexual immorality, and marries another woman commits adultery."

Chapter 16: Divorce: Like Getting Up from a Nasty Fall

After the divorce, I tried to find my way back, but it was a real struggle. I found myself with three children at 33 years old with no husband. I tried not to think about life without him, but Carl did not make it easy. We had arrangements and agreements in the divorce agreement, but it seemed like he was always involved in some aspect of my life, despite all of that. He always used the children as an excuse to wiggle his way into whatever he could. I just wanted him to go somewhere and get a life. I needed real digestible tools to navigate through my broken life. That tool came when I realized that when life and circumstances throw you off track, you always find your way back by trusting in the Lord.

I threw myself into my work, my children, and my trust in a risen Savior. About a year after Carl and I divorced, I went into remission. That was the real storm after the calm; yes, I said it just as I meant to say it. I was in and out of the hospital; in more than out. My sister in Delaware all but took over the care of my children, and my sister who lived in New York was at my house every weekend. Estheree, now married with a little girl of her own, was now living far away from me in Houston, Texas. The distance did not stop her. She was there for me every step of the way, even before the divorce. Whenever she could manage it and got time off from work, she would leave her daughter with her husband and come spend time with me. Carl's parents loved the children dearly and they loved me as well, but we sort of let them take a step back as much as we could when it came to taking care of me. During the summer, the children would go down South for a while, staying at my sister's house in town because it was a lot of responsibility for my parents who were getting older.

Carl would come if whoever was at the house taking care of me would let him, but he never stopped calling and making provision for the children and me. When I was in the hospital, he would come three times a day, if I would agree to let him in my room. One day I was lying in my hospital bed looking out the window at the beautiful foliage. My door opened and I didn't look because I thought it was one of the nurses. Then I heard a voice that was quite familiar say, "Oh, she's asleep and I don't want to wake her up." It was Carl, so I closed my eyes. He walked around the bed and stroked my almost bald head. He kneeled beside the bed. I thought to myself, is this déjà vu all over again? He prayed the most touching prayer, saying that he would do anything, if God would just allow me to get better because he loved me that much. That told the whole story.

I was soon out of the hospital and in time, I was much, much better. Carl's parents had a very dear friend who had been a private duty nurse for years. Her husband had just died, and she sold her house and moved into a small condo downtown; however she spent most of her time with them. They arranged for her to come and live with me during the week, so my children could be at home. She cared for the children, picked them up from school, and transported them to their after-school activities. However, Carl would always stop by on his way to work and take them to school every morning and sometimes take them to the after-school activities.

After about three years, I eventually went back to work in 1987. By that time my company had merged again, and it was now operating under a new name. Unlike before, that 40-minute drive seemed like nothing. I got my life back to normal and I was even talking to Carl again like he was an old friend. He even came over to dinner from time to time. We both thought it was good for the children. The children and I always got into church for the morning service early, unlike Carl who was late every Sunday. When he came in, he would scan the sanctuary until he spotted us. No matter how crowded our pew was, he would manage to squeeze in beside us, even if he had to step across five or 10 pairs of feet to get there. Clarissa asked him one day, "Daddy, how do you always know where we are sitting in church?" He replied, "I can find your mother's hats no matter how many are in there because hers are always the prettiest in the place, just like her."

As much as he loved politics, he never pursued another elected office and, to my knowledge, he never ever dated anybody. If he did, he kept it from his parents because if they knew they would have told it and if they didn't my brother-in-law would have. He became close to Carl when I was very ill. Carl was always at his house visiting with our kids and he sort of felt sorry for Carl. He did not approve of what Carl had done but he would often jokingly tell me, "The man has been hurting for a long time, and his heart has broken and fallen on the ground." I never dated anybody either and didn't even think about it. At the time I felt that I had no love for anybody else, because I had given it all to Carl a long time ago.

One summer, when my children were teenagers, they went on a trip with Carl to southern California. While they were gone, I took some vacation time and went home to visit my parents. It just so happened that Shawn was home that week, too. One day I went to the grocery store for my mommy and he was the first person I saw when I got out of the car. I had not seen him in years and the years had treated him well, because although he had aged, it made him look more mature and handsome. The weather was hot, and I was wearing a pair of capris and a sleeveless shell, like when I was in high school. Although my hair had grown back, it was very thin, and it was pulled back in a ponytail. I know we hugged for five minutes before he stepped back from me and said, "You look just like you did 25 years ago. You have not aged one bit."

Shawn invited himself to dinner that night, As I got ready to drive off, I told him to be there promptly at 6 for dinner. He jokingly said, "Well, I guess your father won't ask me to leave if I stay too long tonight like he used to do."

After dinner, we sat at the dining room table talking for hours. He expressed his sorrow about my divorce and my illness, admitting that he really wanted to come visit me, but was not quite sure what to do or say when he got there. I told him that I was thankful for the cards, flowers, and gifts he had sent. I also told him that my ex was in his neck of the woods as we spoke. He laughed and said he was glad that he was not in California then, because he might have to look Carl up and punch him in the face. He also told me the stories of his love life and that he had been serious twice and thought about marriage at least once, but his career had always come first. "Now," he said, "I realize more and more what I have been missing by not getting married." We talked about old times and the memories. I saw him every day after that until he left that Saturday morning. He promised that I would be seeing a lot more of him when I went home to Delaware. After he left that night, I looked back over the 11 years since Carl and I were divorced and the pain from years of illness. I could not help but think to myself, "Marriage is good, but Shawn, you might be better off single."

Sure enough, about a week after going back home, Shawn called, and we talked for a long time. After that initial call, we talked several times a week. He often told me how lonely he was and how he realized that he made a big mistake, by giving me up in high school. I reminded him that he did not give me up and he would have me as a friend forever. However, I never expressed to him that I was lonely, and I never encouraged him to be anything other than my friend. He flew out from California several times in the next year to see me and invited me to come out so we could take the children to Disneyland. Estheree would always say, "I'm not telling you how to live your life, but if you don't start dating somebody, you will never get over Carl and he will always be in the picture."

My sisters and I tried to get home as often as we could to check on my parents because my daddy had been diagnosed with leukemia. He was doing fine but was very frail. I couldn't help but look at him and Mommy and think how they kept the flame burning for all those years. One weekend, Carl even used my father as an excuse (so I thought) to drive the children and me down to see him, telling me he had planned to visit him that weekend anyway and it would be foolish for us to drive two cars. He and Christopher sat in the front seat and the girls and I sat in back. I slept most of the trip there. While there, that Saturday evening, I sat in the oversized chair in the living room that my daddy had made his memorial retirement chair, after he retired. I thought to myself, "Boy, it takes a real man to fill this chair." Just as I was finishing the thought, my daddy walked into the room. I immediately started to get up, but he motioned me to stay put. He slowly sat down on the sofa across the room. Shortly after he was seated, Carl entered the room and closed the door behind him. I thought, "Now what is he up to? I can't even have a little peace with my daddy." It turned out that day in 1997, in my parents' living room, was one I will always remember.

My daddy said in a voice stronger than I had heard from him in years, "Come on in, Carl, and take a seat. I have been waiting for this all week." I looked puzzled, wondering how did he know that both of us would be here? "Yes, I have something to say to the both of you," he continued. Then I realized that this is a set up. Out of respect for my daddy, I didn't leave the room. This is what he said to us:

"I never condoned what you did to my daughter, Carl, and I was madder than a wet hen when I first heard about it, but I never took sides. I didn't try to tell you Bev, one way or the other what you should do because a husband and wife should solve their own problems. The Bible says husband and wife should confess their sins to one another and pray for one another, that you may be healed because the prayer of a righteous person has great power as it is working.

After all," he said, "that is what your mother and I have done all these years. An old proverb says that hatred stirs up strife, but love covers all offenses. I prayed that somehow the love you two had for each other would help you solve your problems, with the help of the Lord. I can't really know if you have solved your problems, but I am thankful that you are civil to each other and can act like you weren't raised by wolves. I want both of you to promise me that you will stop tearing yourselves apart inside, unnecessarily. Either you get back together, or you go on and build a new life for yourselves. Your mother and I have been right here in this same house almost more years than you have been alive, Bev. Everything is still the same except a couple of remodels. I can get up and look down that tree-lined path and have no regrets. That is what I want the two of you to be able to do...have no regrets about something you could have fixed and didn't. I am preparing to go home, and I look down that path more often now, and I love the memories we made. I am also proud of the legacy I will leave behind. I mean what I say, I don't want to leave here with the two of you unhappy like this."

With that, he got up and left the room and closed the door again, behind him. Carl got up, came over and squeezed down in my daddy's big chair beside me, forcing me to almost be sitting on his lap. He said, "Bev, you know I will always love you and I will do whatever it takes to make you happy." He held me for a long time before either of us said anything. Then he told me my father had called him last week and asked him to come this weekend. "Honestly," he said, "I did not know why he wanted me to come, and that is the truth." I told him that I believed him. I also told him that I loved him with every fiber of my being and I would always love him, but the sun had set on our marriage and it is best if we just support each other in the future each of us chooses. He kissed me on the cheek and said, "If that is what you want, that is what we will do." We sat there for a long time holding each other until Clarissa came busting in asking, "What are you all doing in here with the door closed?

Getting up from a divorce was, metaphorically speaking, just like getting up from a nasty fall. First, before walking straight ahead, I had to make sure that I could stand, balance myself, and navigate the path again. At 47 years old, none of that had been easy. After that talk with my daddy, I was sure that both Carl and I could move on, with our hands in God's hand.

GOLDEN NUGGETS FOR GROWTH #16

I made promises before God that I would love and honor and cherish my husband until one of us died. We both promised to take care of each other until death do us part. That did not happen! I loved being married to the man I married, and I put my heart and soul into my marriage day and night, good times, children time, and family time. When things went wrong, all of that went out the door. I think now of what I did not think of then. When two people love each other, they should try everything they know to work it out, but unfortunately that did not happen with us, and it seldom happens with any couple. In my marriage, I put love in the back seat and stood solely on morals and principles. My advice to couples who are contemplating divorce is if you really love your mate, ask yourself if your love outweighs the offense that's causing the problem. If you think it does, fight with that love. It's usually too late when you get down the road and have nothing left but a heart full of regrets and would haves, could haves, and should haves.

Generally, a couple will state a reason for getting a divorce, but often that is not the underlying reason. They may shout it from the rooftop that they hate the mate, when in actuality, they love the mate as much as they always did. It is the offense that was committed that they hate. They don't know how to process that reality and what it means for their future. Hindsight is 20/20, and when you see what should have been, in the rearview mirror, usually it's too late.

In the years since my divorce, things have changed for me. Miracles have happened. I have learned amazing lessons about life and love and joy and peace and contentment. Along with those things, I often wonder if I made a mistake. Should I have let love work it out? I don't know the answer to that. But what I have earned is that I had to take my life back and make it good again and heal, after the divorce. How did I do that? Well, I worked with several things: I moved on and let the past be the past; I focused on things that I could now control, the only one that should actually dwell on what happened is the guilty party, and I was not guilty; and I realized that what I do with my future is up to me.

God has a way of reaching into the darkest of places and shining a light that you never knew was there.

WHAT SCRIPTUE SAYS ABOUT MOVING ON:

John 14:13 (KJV)--"Whatever you ask in my name, this I will do, that the Father may be glorified in the Son."

Philippians 3:13-14 (NIV)--"Brothers and sisters, I do not consider myself yet to have taken hold of it. But one thing I do: Forgetting what is behind and straining toward what is ahead, I press on toward the goal to win the prize for which God has called me heavenward in Christ Jesus."

Isaiah 43:18 (NIV)--"Remember ye not the former things, neither consider the things of old. "Forget the former things; do not dwell on the past."

Chapter 17: Moving On

After going back home, the conversation between my daddy, Carl and me stuck in my head. One thing that stayed with me and kept resonating in my brain that my daddy said to us was, "I want both of you to promise me that you will stop tearing yourselves apart inside, unnecessarily. Either you get back together, or you go on and build a new life for yourselves." I pondered it and prayed for closure and then put the thought aside. One Saturday morning about five or six months later, I was sitting in my den reading my daily devotional when a feeling of peace and calm came over me. It was the same kind of safe feeling I felt when was a little girl, hiding under the window from the hobo. I stood up and said, "I heard you, Daddy and Lord, I hear you now. It is time to move on."

Later that same afternoon, Darlene came over to say goodbye before she went back to England. She had lived there for about five years and this trip home was the first time I had seen her in as many years. We were sitting in the kitchen having coffee and recalling our college days when the phone rang. When I said, "Hello." the voice on the other end said, "Daddy is gone." It was my sister from home. Daddy had just died, and they hadn't even removed him from the house yet. I asked to speak to Mommy, but she said, "Not right now, the nurse is giving her a sedative." I told her that I would call her right back and would be there as soon I got straight. I sat down at the table and told Darlene what had happened. We called my children and then she called her parents.

When we got settled, I told her that I knew my daddy waited until I made up my mind to keep the promise he asked me to make. I had only made up my mind that morning and, somehow, he knew It was then that he felt it was now time to go on to glory. I had only made up my mind this morning and, somehow, he knew. He must have been pleased and knew it was alright to go on home. Darlene drove me to my sister's house there in Delaware. As we consoled each other, we said that there's no need to cry about Daddy's death because he carried out his task, but he would want us to celebrate his life. By that time, Carl was there. What he said made me know that he had decided what he needed to do also (the Carl I knew would be trying to use this as an opportunity to move back in with me). But it was different. He said, "I won't get in your way, but whatever you need done, I will be at your disposal." Darlene told me that she would take care of the children and everything there that needed to be done because she would not be going back to England until after the funeral. So, the next morning, my sister in New York and I took a flight home. My other sister and her family came a few days later along with Carl, Darlene, and the children.

Shawn arrived on the day of the funeral. As we assembled at the house, both Carl and Shawn came pushing through the crowd to take my arm. Estheree, as usual, came to the rescue. She told them, "Now, this is what we are going to do. Christopher, you get your mother. Carl, you get Carla; and Shawn, you get Clarissa and you all are going to support each other." I was so proud to play my father's favorite hymn at his funeral. I'm not bragging, but I really played that song as the choir sang "Amazing Grace." It was almost as if his hands were in my hands. I felt even prouder when one of his dear friends came up to me when we were leaving, hugged me, and said, "You played that just like your father would have." The procession took Daddy back by our house on the way to the cemetery, riding slowly down the path lined on both sides with trees. I know he would have liked that, my mommy said.

When I got back to Delaware, I put my all into work and looking after my children. I did not socialize a lot, but I was very involved in church and community activities. I went back to Delaware State to finish my master's. Shawn called a couple of times a week and flew out from California about once per month. We had grown very close and when he would visit, we talked for hours. I counted him as one of my best friends. However, I made it clear that I just wanted friendship and not a relationship. Carl had started to see someone, too, the principal from the high school where he taught when he first graduated from college. He was always quick to tell everybody that the two of them are just friends, strictly friends.

When I finished my master's, my children and my sisters had a graduation party for me. My brother even brought Mommy up and we insisted that he stop frequently so she could rest. She looked so pretty in her navy-blue suit, her favorite color. Shawn was already in New York on a business trip, so he came over for the weekend. Carl also came but did not bring his friend with him. When my brother-in-law asked him why his lady friend wasn't with him, he said, "She's not my lady friend, but just a friend. She is somebody I just put on my arm sometimes to keep the women away," he laughed. Throughout the evening, every chance he got, he would say, "This is another special day and I am so proud of my wife." One of my friends from work said to me after he had repeated it about three times, that she thought we had been divorced for years. I said, "We have been, and he is my EX husband," loud enough for him to hear. He just laughed and said, "Don't mind her, she will always be MY wife."

After the party was over and everybody had either gone home or upstairs to bed, Shawn and I sat at the dining room table and talked. Without warning, he kissed me before I could protest. Then he said, "That was for a reason and don't say a word." He pulled a small box from his coat pocket and opened it. I was so shocked that I couldn't say a word. He got down on one knee and asked me to marry him. I hugged him real tight and then I said, "Our friendship is too beautiful to mess up with marriage." He told me that he loved me and was ready to make that commitment because he has given me up once and he was not about to do it again. It was so difficult to make him understand that we both knew then, as we do now, that we cannot mess up this beautiful relationship by getting romantically involved. I loved him dearly, but I knew that I could not marry him. Finally, we came to a mutual understanding. When he went back to California, we did not talk as much as we had in the past. He told me that he, too, had thrown himself into his work. However, we continued to be friends.

The next year, in 1999, my mother passed away. She had a massive heart attack and died before she got to the hospital. A couple of days after the funeral, Estheree came over from her aunt's house before heading back to Houston. She said, "Guess who I saw this morning?" Before I could ask who, she said, "Kirby's brother. He wants us to come by his father's old garage before we go back home." We decided to go that afternoon. When we walked into the garage, he pulled a canvas off the old pink Pontiac. The front tag was a picture of the T-Twelve. He explained that he had found the picture in the glove compartment years ago and decided to have it transformed into a license plate. The car was pristine, just as clean and shiny as it was when we were in high school. It was truly a treat to see that car again and it brought back memories.

Several years after my mother died, my sister who lived in Delaware was also diagnosed with leukemia. She did very well at first, but after a while, we could see her fading. She died a year later. We had a memorial service in Wilmington for her and then took her home for a funeral. By this time, Carl had moved on and so had Shawn, but in addition to my family, I was glad that I still had both as friends. They provided so much inspiration and support during those dark years. Shawn didn't come to the funeral, but he called to extend his condolences and to make sure that we were OK.

As time passed, conversations between Shawn and me were not so frequent. He called me one day and told me that he had met someone while on a business trip. He said that he was very fond of her but was not ready to take the plunge just yet. I wished him well and he cautioned me not to spend the remainder of my life alone. In 2003, Carl moved to Dover and started toying with the idea of maybe running for public office again. Everybody seemed to be moving on, even my children. I had time on my hands, so I went back to school again.

GOLDEN NUGGETS FOR GROWTH #17

Don't fall for the lie that you can't enjoy life until all your problems have been resolved. In this world you have trouble, but in God you will always have peace. Starting over in life only requires that you just put it all together and move on, being willing to let go of what isn't working or what's holding you back. When creating the life, you want, set realistic and attainable goals so that you can work toward your dreams because there will always be problems. Make time for fun and leisure activities to bring meaning and enjoyment to your life. Change is the only constant.

Everyone without a doubt goes through changes in their lives whether it be a physical state of literal aging, a mental state of emotional maturity, or regression, in some cases. They all nonetheless signify change, yet some of us seem to embrace it better than others. I finally did.

I must admit that when it comes to change, I have never been the most accepting. Don't get me wrong. I love a challenge and am not one to sit still and stay stagnant. Yet, the soothing feeling of being in my "comfort zone" is also one that makes embracing change a lot harder, especially when the change I'm about to make is not easy, and perhaps even something I dislike. My ex-husband was one of those changes that I found very hard with which to deal. I loved him very much, yet I knew I couldn't be his wife anymore.

Often when we feel insecure, we consult others, so we feel better about our plan or our preparation for a transformation. But your life is YOUR life. Move on and people will grow with you. Those that don't perhaps aren't meant to be in your life in the first place. You don't need to tell other people or ask them what they think you should do! That is really between you and God.

WHAT SCRIPUTURE SAYS ABOUT MOVING ON:

Romans 8:18 (ESV)--"For I consider that the sufferings of this present time are not worth comparing with the glory that is to be revealed to us."

Jeremiah 29:11 (ESV)--"For I know the plans I have for you, declares the Lord, plans for welfare and not for evil, to give you a future and a hope."

Philippians 3:14 (ESV)--"I press on toward the goal for the prize of the upward call of God in Christ Jesus."

Isaiah 43:18-19 (ESV)--"Remember not the former things, nor consider the things of old. Behold, I am doing a new thing; now it springs forth, do you not perceive it? I will make a way in the wilderness and rivers in the desert."

2 Corinthians 5:7 (NIV)--"For we walk by faith, not by sight."

Chapter 18: A Sharp Turn in the Curve

One day I looked up in 2013 and realized that it had been 35 or so years since my divorce from Carl. It seemed like yesterday when my oldest child, Christopher, took his first step. I remembered Carl saying, he takes strides just like his daddy. But it was not yesterday, and I found myself in this big house all by myself. The children still came often, with their families, which was a joy because I love the grands--three of them, full of energy.

I seldom spent much time at home anymore. When I was not at the university, I was up at the church office or in the neighborhood taking up some worthwhile cause. I didn't like to think of myself as retired, although I was. Most of my girlfriends had retired about the same time I did. Even Estheree had retired and I thought she would work until she was 80. Well, she is not exactly retired, because she and her husband owned a bed and breakfast in Houston. She loved it and cherished every minute of taking care of it and the overnight guests they always had stay there. Elizabeth retired and moved back home because she said that country living was the best way to settle down. She always said her "out time" was when she drove the 35 miles to the city a couple of times a week and found things to keep her busy while she was there, and she also kept busy as the choir director at the First Baptist Church in town. I think everybody in town was just waiting from her to move back so she could do that. For me, I just didn't consider myself as being retired, because I took a part-time position in the research department at the university, which keeps me busy a few days per week along with my post-graduate endeavors.

It was getting toward summer vacation time. I really did not want to go anywhere that year. After all, I had already planned to go to the National Baptist Convention in Fort Worth, Texas, in August. My pastor's wife and I were going together because Pastor had over-extended himself and committed to a project in Haiti for a month, the same time as the convention. His wife repeatedly said to him, "I told you to keep your calendar up to date and if you had listened to me, this would not have happened." Anyway, when Estheree learned that we were coming to Texas, she talked me into a vacation, just the two of us, the week after the convention. I could almost hear the ideas plotting in her head saying, "You see we can go down to Cancun and take in some sun. It will be good for us, and Barry can take care of the B&B by himself while I am gone." So, I let her talk me into it.

For an entire week before the convention, I packed and unpacked because I couldn't decide what I wanted to wear, which hat to take, with which outfit. Then there was the added stress of putting together something for the vacation in Cancun. So, I finally said, I will just ship my vacation things to Estheree. Then I would mix and match a few pieces and hats for the convention and anything else I needed, I would buy when I got to Texas. That sounded like a plan.

The pastor's wife (Doris Tate) and I had a truck load of luggage to get checked at the airport, but we got it all done and boarded the plane for Texas. She and I were doing a mini-presentation at one of the scheduled workshops on the closing day of the convention, so we talked about the final touch to the PowerPoint we had put together once we were on the plane.

The convention was outstanding with a lot of activity and interaction. The second day we were there, Sister Tate and I were sitting in one of the little cafés in the convention center, drinking coffee. My back was to the door and I heard someone say, "It is so good to see you." When I looked up there was a tall dark gentleman standing there with one hand in his pocket. Then somebody called him, and he said he would see her later and rushed off. I just gazed after him. Sister Tate was talking to me and I didn't even hear her. She touched my arm, "Bev, don't you hear me?" "I'm sorry, who was that man?" I asked. She told me that it was the Rev. William Alford and she tried to make me know him because he lived in Wilmington. "With all your getting around, I am surprised that you don't know him," she said. I told her that I would have remembered him if I had seen him before. She just laughed and started talking about something else, but my mind was still stuck on that man standing there with one hand in his pocket.

That night when we went to dinner, he was already at the restaurant with a group of other convention attendees. When we were seated, he came over. Sister Tate introduced him to me. He put out his hand to greet me and it felt like a velvet glove when our fingers touched and he said, "We have to stop these chance meetings and really take time and sit down and chat." Then he said that he had seen in the program that we were presenting on Thursday and he would make a point of coming to our session. When we got to the area to set up on Thursday, there was a note to me, not Sister Tate, that he was so sorry but he had an emergency board meeting and could not attend our session, but would like to see me later.

The convention closed that evening and we were scheduled to leave the next morning; Sister Tate to fly back to Wilmington and me to Houston. However, Estheree and her husband drove the four-hour trip to pick me up instead. We left right after the closing session and I never got to see him the next day. A few days later, when Sister Tate was back at home, I got a call from her saying that Reverend Alford was on her flight home and wanted to know where I was. After explaining that I had gone on to Mexico on vacation, he asked her about me. She didn't tell him much except that I was not married. That, she said, was all he wanted to know anyway. He also asked if she thought I would mind if he got my number from her and she gave it to him. She called me to give me a heads-up that I might get a call.

When we got back from Cancun, I stayed another week at Estheree's B&B in Houston before going home. I flew home on a Monday. It was mid-afternoon when I got there, and my nephew picked me up because I had shipped boxes of "stuff" back and needed some way to get them home and unloaded. We put the boxes on the sun porch and the suitcases upstairs. I told him that he could come back and get them upstairs for me later. I had been gone for three week and that September afternoon was as warm as it was when I left in August. I had never been so ready to take a shower and just relax. I took a shower and wrapped myself in my favorite terrycloth robe. Just as I sat down with a cold drink the phone rang. It was him! The very first thing he said after we greeted each other and got through the particulars was "I have been trying to reach you for a week." I told him that I had been on vacation in Mexico. He replied that he knew that, but I was supposed to be home a week ago. I knew that Sister Tate had told him this, but I just wanted to tease him a little. And how do you know that, I asked and for that matter, how do you know anything about me?

His deep voice lowered a bit, sending chills right through me, saying OK, let's start again. "I asked your friend about you and she told me where you were and that you would be gone for a week. I didn't want to interfere with your vacation, so I waited a week and then I called, not once but three or four times," he said. I went ahead and explained everything to him and told him I was sorry that I hadn't been home when he called so many times. Then he explained his many phone calls, telling me that he had committed to taking Reverend Tate's place in Haiti, once he returns. "I thought you were coming back last week so I could have some time to talk to you before I left and that is why I was calling so much. You see, I am due to leave in a few days," he said. "I don't believe this," I thought. Here is someone I am dying to get to know and he is on his way to Haiti for a month. I guess this was my season to be shocked and disappointed, because at every curve lately there has been a sharp turn.

When I told him that I had just gotten home, the enthusiasm seemed to have disappeared from his voice. "I was going to ask you out to dinner, but I know you must be very tired. I am so sorry, I just didn't think," he said. Instead of saying what was feeling, I replied by saying, "Thanks, but no thanks. I have been eating out for more than three weeks and going to a restaurant is the last thing that I want to do tonight," I told him. "That's fine how rude of me holding you on the phone all this time when you must be exhausted. Perhaps, we can talk tomorrow," he said. I sensed what I had done and tried to fix it by saying, "I've enjoyed talking to you." "Well, you get some rest and I will talk to you later," he said and hung up.

After hanging up the phone, I decided that I would take a little nap, but that just did not happen. I said to myself, "Bev, you blew that one good, didn't you?" I paced the floor feeling like I felt that day when I saw Carl in Darlene's dorm room, but about 10 notches higher. Then I remembered, the Lord asked us to invite Him into our moments by talking with Him about everything that concerns us, whatever is on our minds. I knew that I had left the past behind me and I didn't want to go back there but had unintentionally sabotaged what could have taken me forward. I said, "Lord, you said that whatever I am facing, you will help me handle it better. I am depending on you to do what I cannot do by myself." With that said, a calm came over me and I sat down in my favorite chair and had my cold glass of lemonade and tried to visualize what the reverend really looked like, as I had only seen him a couple of times briefly at the convention.

I went out the next day to take care of some errands, which took most of the day. When I got home, I talked to each of my children, catching them up on what had happened the three weeks I was gone. The next day, I headed to the university early in the morning to get a new research project up and running for several graduate students. The entire time I was thinking that the signal that I sent when we talked on the phone surely turned him off. On Thursday, I went up to the church to work on a project, and I ran into Sister Tate. She gave me an envelope as soon as I walked in. I laid it on the desk, and she commented, "I thought you were interested in him. Aren't you going to read it?" I picked it up and opened it. It was a note from the reverend.

The note said, "I am sorry that I bothered you. I wanted very much to talk to you and see you before I left, but you didn't return my calls, so I guess you are not interested. You can't blame a man for trying. Regards, William Alford." I looked at her with questioning eyes. She said that he had come by the house this morning before he left to see her husband and asked me to give it to you. I said, "Before he left for where?" "He's gone. Each one of a group of seven preachers were taking a sabbatical in Haiti for a month to help on the mission field. Now that Pastor Tate is back, it is his turn," she said. "He will be in Florida for a few weeks at seminars before going on to Haiti." Then I remembered that he told me that. "But what does he mean I didn't return his calls?" I said. She then said, "He was disappointed that he had called you every day since you've been back and asked you to call him when you got in and you didn't." "I've been busy the past couple of days and I didn't know he had been calling," I said. Well, there goes that sharp turn in the curve again, I thought. When I got home I checked my messages and sure enough he had called twice on Tuesday and three times on Wednesday and each time, he asked me to call him when I got in because he had something to tell me.

I didn't hear anymore from him, but I kept thinking a month is not a long time. When he gets back, I can explain. I thought about him every day. Then one day in early October, Sister Tate and I were talking, and she mentioned some of the things Pastor Tate had learned during his month-long sabbatical. I said, "Reverend Alford will be back in November. I guess he will have learned a lot, also." She said, "Well no, he will be back in December. He took a double assignment, because one of the other pastors couldn't follow him because of a family problem." I was crushed! I walked out of the room so she wouldn't see me tear up. Later in November, she told me that her husband had gotten a letter from him and he had asked for my mailing address. That was the best news I had heard in a while. Now, at least I could anticipate hearing from him.

Around the end of November, I received that long-awaited letter. In the letter he said that he knew I was not interested, but he just could not get me out of his thoughts. After working on the mission fields of Haiti, he said he realized that he needed to at least tell me how he felt because he believed that God had his hand on that chance encounter back at the convention in August. I read the letter again and then a third time. I made up my mind to write him back, thinking that, at 63, I am getting to old to spend the rest of my life alone. So, I wrote, and I told him that I, too, had been thinking about him since he left. I told him that I never got his messages until after he was gone. In addition, I told him that I was very much interested in getting to know him...and we continued to write.

December came and then came Christmas. I learned that it would be December 31 before he arrived back in Florida for debriefing. Another sharp turn in the curve. Four months...a long wait! The day he arrived, he called and said that he would be flying into LaGuardia on January 2. I really would have been OK with the drive over to New York City to pick him up, but arrangements had already been made for one of the deacons from his church to meet him. It was late afternoon when he got to Wilmington, and he called me right away to tell me he was home and would be over that night, if it was OK with me. I agreed that I would fix dinner. I had waited four months to see and talk to him and I was not about to wait another day, if I didn't have to.

GOLDEN NUGGETS FOR GROWTH #18

Love at first sight. We hear that a lot, but is it possible for two strangers to really fall in love the first time they see each ther? When we look at what the Bible says about true Christian love (1 Corinthians 13:4-13), we can see that "love at first sight" is not at all the same. You can't love someone in a deep, meaningful way at first sight because you know nothing about that person. If that were true you wouldn't fall out of love with that person, no matter what. Although I thought I fell in love at first sight, not once but two times, does not make it so. I just had an intense reaction that I imagined, which is not love at all. The stuff that love is made of doesn't happen in the first moment you look at someone. One can, however, have a connection with another person when you first see him and that may develop into love.

1 Corinthians 13:4-7 (NIV) says, "Love is patient, love is kind. It does not envy, it does not boast, it is not proud. It does not dishonor others, it is not self-seeking, it is not easily angered, it keeps no record of wrongs. Love does not delight in evil but rejoices with the truth. It always protects, always trusts, always hopes, always perseveres."

Dealing with the sharp turns in the curves:

As you intentionally seek to live a Christ-centered life, Satan will take notice and use every trick to get you to fall away from your intentional walk with the Lord. In our walk we will struggle and fail, because we are human. However, we have a Savior who walks with us. He loved us enough to die for us while we were still sinners.

Because of this great love, we can rest assured that even when we do mess up and fall, God will provide us a way out of those traps. Those traps come in the form of sharp turns in the curves. God will cover us with His love and forgiveness and straighten the curves.

If we depend on God, He is our hope and our salvation. We need never be fearful of wrecking in those curves. We need to stop doubting and believe that God has a plan for us even if we can't comprehend it at that time. We must stay faithful when we don't feel like it or when we are uncertain. When things become more central to our lives than the Lord, we must take a step back. We must pray, humble ourselves, and be patient as we move forward as we rely on Him and His strength, not our own, as we move toward a more intentional Christian life.

WHAT SCRIPTURE SAYS ABOUT PRIDE, FEAR, IMPATIENCE, SELFISHNESS, AND DOUBT:

Proverbs 16:18 (KJV)--"Pride goes before destruction, and a haughty spirit before a fall."

2 Timothy 1:7 (ESV)--"God gave us a spirit not of fear but of power and love and self-control."

Psalm 27:14 (NKJV)--"Wait on the LORD; Be of good courage, And He shall strengthen your heart; Wait, I say, on the LORD!"

Galatians 5:16 (ESV)--"So I say, walk by the Spirit, and you will not gratify the desires of the flesh."

James 1:6-8 (NKJV)--"But let him ask in faith, with no doubting, for the one who doubts is like a wave of the sea that is driven and tossed by the wind. For that person must not suppose that he will receive anything from the Lord; he is a double-minded man, unstable in all his ways."

Chapter 19: The Man in the Sophisticated Brown Hat

It all started to materialize on that cold January evening in 2014. I had been anticipating seeing my new admirer since I got the phone call earlier that day. Even though we only talked briefly on the phone it was so refreshing to actually hear his voice. It's kind of hard to explain, but it seemed as if God had already given me the vision. It was almost as if I had dreamed him into existence. Somehow, I knew he would become a part of my life because it had already been destined. So, you can see why that January evening will always be etched in my mind. It is almost as if I had dreamed him into life...again things had been made right for me.

When that face-to-face meeting was finally about to happen, I displayed more of the characteristics of a schoolgirl than that of a mature woman. My emotions were all over the place and I was ridiculously falling all over myself. I don't know how I managed to cook dinner without messing it up and burning it up. Racing from closet to closet, I could not wrap my mind around what would be the best thing to wear for that face-to-face encounter...should I wear something dressy, maybe all black to make me look slimmer?; No, a casual pair of slacks and a sweater will do the trick. Yes, something simple—slacks and a plain sweater will be best, I finally decided. All of this was so out of character for me. Never had I acted this way about anybody.

When my telephone rang and I heard this deep stately voice on the other end of the line say, "I'm in your driveway," I froze. "What am I going to do now?" I asked myself out loud. But before I could think, my mind raced off and I looked in the foyer mirror to take one last inventory of my appearance as my doorbell rang. Then I hesitantly opened the door.

When the door opened, I didn't see what I remembered or what I had turned over in my head a thousand times about what his face looked like. What I saw was so much more. What I did see under a brown hat, was a shy smile, radiating from one of the most handsome faces that I had seen in recent years. A strong mannish hello found its way through a pair of lips that I wanted to claim one day and, honestly, I don't know how I replied. I just stood there glued to that spot for what seemed like an eternity. Then I got my wits about myself and invited him in. I took his coat and that memorable brown hat and deposited them in the hall closet as I concealed my awkwardness. As I placed the coat and hat in the closet, I gently stroked that brown hat slightly, thinking, man does he wear that well. I was almost afraid to turn and face him. When I did, he was just standing there with his left hand in his pocket. For fear of making a fool of myself, I invited him to the sofa and slid haphazardly onto the couch beside him. The cushion buckled underneath me and when my leg touched his, I couldn't distinguish the soft cushion from the sleekness of the upper thigh of his right leg.

I said to myself, now this is high-schoolish behavior. Sure, you are a bit rusty at this; well a lot rusty at this...it has been almost 36 years but get a hold of yourself.

Once we started to talk, I could barely stay focused for gazing at him...gazing not because I wanted to look at him, but more because I couldn't believe that I had invited him over and he was here in my living room. I think he sensed my uneasiness because he stopped talking and looked at me with a questioning WHAT, on his face. That deep, take-charge voice was driving me crazy.

Then, it was time for dinner. As he stepped into the bathroom to wash his hands and refresh, I got the food on the table. I still could not figure out what it was that was so magical about that night—was it the fact that everything I had seen or envisioned about him was right there before me, or was it that as we talked I began to realize that we had so much in common. I think it was simply that I had not been in a frank conversation with a man in so many years that I was shocked into unreality. Whatever it was, I was glad that he was there, and I hated that the time just seemed to melt away. During dinner, he talked more about his stay in Haiti. He was such a gentleman and I was so happy that I had finally met him, officially. But why wouldn't he be a gentleman, he's a preacher! Who would expect any less of him?

After dinner, we had coffee in the den. We spent about two hours talking about ourselves, nothing else. The night went so fast and it seemed that he was gone almost as fast as he had come, but I knew one thing, I had confirmation that I had fallen in love that night. After he left, I went about the remainder of the night in slow motion. As I said my prayers and slipped under the covers, I once again thanked God for sending him my way. As my head touched my pillow, I could hear his deep, commanding voice ringing in my ears, and I could see him standing there at my front door in that brown hat.

That night, and the months ahead went leisurely by However, I always paused on the second day of each month to think about that first night at my house, with him wearing the sophisticated brown hat. Along with those thoughts, the lyrics to the song "Every Day I Love You More" pierced my heart and drove home exactly what I was feeling in my heart, which goes like this…" don't know, but I believe that some things are meant to be and that he'll make me a better me every day I love him." Sort of like the Comforter who has been my companion all these years. I feel that we are the very best and I will be blessed every day I'm with him.

For the first time since the years when I was married, I felt special, really special, on Valentine's Day. The man in the brown hat made me feel that way and it was on that day that he became the true love in my life. He appeared at my door with chocolate candy (not my favorite but because he gave it to me, it was that day) and a card. The card was simple and did not mention anything about love, but love radiated through it and I felt the love as I opened and read it. At that moment, I felt like running, screaming through the neighborhood.

As the months went on and winter turned to spring a feeling of magic seemed to be covering my life; correction, more like blessings covering my life. My children liked him, Estheree had started planning a trip so she could come and meet him, and my sister was suspicious of him, saying you don't find a man as nice as him just hanging around. Yes, life was good.

We set some ground rules, not that we needed to, but nevertheless we did. With the rules in tow, we went on a trip during spring break to one of the most romantic cities in the South, Charleston, South Carolina. We spent the better part of a week there. He was a perfect gentleman, and we saw a lot of the city and had lots of fun. I came away from that excursion with a renewed understanding of him and with a far better appreciation of who he was. I had finally been given something tangible to hold on to and something to cherish without compromising my morals and values as a person.

Yes, the Rev. William Tyrell Alford was the man I wanted to spend the remainder of my life with. He was one of the sweetest, most considerate individuals I have ever been involved with and I loved him very much. He was also a godly man; a minister and he was practicing what he preached. I didn't think I could be any happier with anybody than I was with him. For years I have asked God to send me a kind and gentle man that would return the love that I had to give; not a man who would be my friend, but a man that would be my man. He did just that and gave me a bonus in the deal, a preacher. Secretly, I have always fantasized about being a preacher's wife, walking proudly beside him and sitting in the congregation watching him as he delivers his messages from the pulpit.

On occasions, I would be absent from Sunday morning service at my church and could be found in the congregation at Mt. Rainer Missionary Baptist Church. When I talked to Estheree on the phone, I would laughingly tell her I was getting practice for when I would become the preacher's wife.

A 60-something-year-old woman should not be acting and feeling like a schoolgirl, but I think it is alright for her to show love and affections because love can be part of your life at any age. Hopefully, we all can be brave, confident, and open to possibilities, and willing to take a chance on letting love into our hearts once more. Such a relationship should not be a power struggle and both parties should recognize the other has something valuable to offer, conversation, companionship, and shared interests. Both should also enjoy each other's company.

Whenever we want to know something about true love though, the first place we should go is to God. How does God show his true love for us? God didn't just tell us that he loves us. He showed his love for us in action. When you meet the right person, I think God will empower you to know the difference between infatuation and real commitment. When you truly begin to love someone, really have agape love, the kind Christ has shown us, you will know it. You will know it because you will find more joy in serving and giving to that person than in being served. Even when you realize you don't need a man to make you happy, you still would like to have someone with whom to share your life, mutual interests, and common views. It is about finding a partnership of equals with a foundation of trust, healthy relationships, boundaries, and mutual respect.

WHAT SCRIPTUE (SAYS ABOUT FINDING SOULMATES:

Colossians 2:2 (NKJV)--"That their hearts may be encouraged, having been knit together in love, and attaining to all the wealth that comes from the full assurance of understanding, resulting in a true knowledge of God's mystery, that is, Christ Himself."

Genesis 2:22 (NASB)--"The LORD God fashioned into a woman the rib which He had taken from the man, and brought her to the man."

Isaiah 34:16 (NASB)—"Seek from the book of the LORD, and read: Not one of these will be missing; None will lack its mate For His mouth has commanded, And His Spirit has gathered them."

Song of Solomon 3:4 (NASB)--"Scarcely had I left them; When I found him whom my soul loves; I held on to him and would not let him go, Until I had brought him to my mother's house, And into the room of her who conceived me."

Psalm 37:4 (NASB)--"Take delight in the Lord, and he will give you the desires of your heart."

James 1:17 (NASB)—"Whatever is good and perfect comes down to us from God our Father, who created all the lights in the heavens."

Chapter 20: Another Turning Point in My Life

I knew I loved William because he was who he was. No matter what I was doing, I never got tired of thinking about or seeing him. I hastened to include him in my prayers, and I thanked God for giving me the opportunity to have him in my life. When good things happened to me during the day, I always have the urge to tell him about them. When bad things happened, I felt better when I shared them with him. His feelings were as important to me as my own. I also knew I loved him because I didn't consider his imperfections as flaws; instead, I thought of them as unique qualities and things I loved about him. My sense of self changed along with my habits and demeanor; changes that others could readily see and spoke about.

The first birthday I celebrated after I met him indicated that he was different. I remember when I was married to Carl, he did some really over-the-top things for my birthday, but this was different in a plain and simple way. I was feeling especially wonderful because both of us had taken the day off to spend it together. I got up that morning and took my time talking to God and thanking him for another day. I was so glad I waited on God, because I believed He gave me what He knew I needed and not what I have been telling Him I didn't want all these years. Anyway, later in the day of July 24, 2015, William arrived with a dozen of the most beautiful red roses I had ever seen and another one of his famous cards. It is so strange that those cards never say anything about love, but I can feel the love as I read them pouring out of every letter of every word. I am sure I know how Cinderella must have felt with the prince at the ball before the clock struck midnight, because I felt just that way with him standing there with those flowers.

He took me out for the afternoon, and it was wonderful. Simple, but the best birthday present I ever wanted to have. You see, when you have walked the walked that I have walked, you learn to appreciate and be thankful for the ordinary things in life. He took me up to Dover, Delaware, and we had a tour of a section of the museum of art. But you know what is so ironic. We toured a section of art history related to a romantic love affair and marriage. I thought that was so special and we both enjoyed it. For dinner, he took me to my favorite restaurant back in Wilmington and I had one of my most favorite things to eat, Mile High Chocolate Cake. Of course, the entrée was good also, but I always concentrate on the dessert. That birthday was very special to me and probably the one I remember most.

I had birthday parties when I was growing up, and my girlfriends would take me out and give me presents after I grew up, and I remember when I was married years ago, my ex-husband would buy me expensive things and give me money for my birthday. That, however, did not mean much to me, because I would have been happier with him just giving of himself. That is exactly what William did, he gave of his time and he showed that he cared although he didn't too often say the words "I love." He once told me that he had problems expressing his feelings, but he hoped his actions showed what he is feeling. They did!

I must admit, I sometimes felt a bit of jealousy, but not the suspiciously mad jealousy that is toxic; the kind that can destroy a relationship. I guess it was a healthy kind of jealousy that I felt, if there is such a thing, that wells up sometimes when he talked about not letting highs and lows in his life influence his emotions or outlook on life. Everybody has highs and lows, but William would let them roll off like water off a duck's back. I was a little jealous of that because I couldn't do that. I did, however, foster a healthy, loving relationship with him tempered with trust and faith and I believed that we could get through anything together. I always worked at making sure that there was freedom in our relationship as I was sure he did, too. For I didn't want to hold too tight and find the relationship starting to crumble, but we still always found time to see each other. Here and there, I would go off for a visit with one of my children or all of them would come for a weekend. He got to know them very well and to my surprise he and my youngest daughter (the die-hard Daddy's girl) really got to be buddies.

He had been talking about his upcoming vacation and he said that it would please him to stay at home and just sleep for a week or two. He always took the month of September each year. One Sunday afternoon, he came over for dinner and we were sitting on the sun porch when he asked me how I would like to vacation with him this year. Immediately, I said that would be lovely, but I am obligated to the university and projects around the community and can't get away for a whole month. Before I could finish, he had a solution. "Well," he said, "Let's go for a week or so and then we can come back, and I can hang around my house and yours for the remainder of the time and catch up on some much overdue reading." He thought, Miami was real nice last September when he stopped there on his way to Haiti and that is an excellent vacation spot. I agreed.

We decided to rent a car and drive down so we could take a detour to my hometown of Coltonville for a day or two so he could meet the rest of my family. Then we could fly back from Miami. It was good to go home again. He got to meet my brother and my sister who lived in town. My brother and his wife lived in our old house and my sister and her family came out from town and we had a nice dinner the last night we were there. He loved the quiet tree-lined path leading up to the house. He told me that he would like to come South and live in a place just like this when

...e retired from the ministry. We drove on to Miami and had a wonderful six days before flying back to Delaware.

When we were in Miami, I found out exactly how he felt. Many years ago, I thought I was in love, but the first rough patch in the road derailed that. Real love shows itself even if the sun is not shining and the day is as gray as an old worn out fox. I have dreamed about what love is a thousand times and I think I have a pretty good grasp on what it is to me. In my past it was loving friendship, then it was loving marriage, but this is different.

As summer turned to fall and then moved on toward winter again, we had a few rocky situations where I had a pity party or two, but as I said before, nothing changes William's attitude because he believed that if you want to, you can work anything out. I, on the other hand, wondered if I was better off before I became interested in someone again.

Several situations did not feel right, and I vowed to walk away and never look back again. One specific time was like déjà vu all over again. I felt a familiar wave of hurt come over me on a Sunday that I had envisioned to be extra special. I went to hear Reverend Alford preach as a guest minister at a friend's church. I thought to myself as I walked in, "God is good, and life is good." He delivered an especially powerful sermon and I was moved to tears of joy and spiritual release. However, immediately after the service, there were real tears of sadness and hurt. One of the parishioners walked over and said, "Congratulations on your engagement, but you look so different from the way you looked last week when Reverend Alford introduced you at our revival." The fact is, I had not been there during revival. I didn't wait for him to come to me. I just turned and walked out the side door. I managed to keep my composure until I reached my car, and then the flood gates opened. Why would he bring someone else to this church and not tell me about it and to whom is he engaged? I said to myself, "I cannot, and I will not go through this again." I prayed a little prayer and went on my way. As I was about to drive off, my cell phone rang. It was him, asking why I left in such a hurry and that he wanted me to wait around for him. I just said I needed to get home and take these shoes off.

As I drove home, I tried to put things in perspective: This man chose me and although he has no obligations to do so, he keeps coming back, so I don't think I have anything to worry about, but I was still puzzled about the engagement part. The lesson here is, hear all sides first, if it's a mix up then thank God for the blessing and work to make that blessing last. You see, the devil has a way of clouding your mind, but you must stay focused on God and his love, mercy and goodness and move past what the devil is trying to do. I have too much God in me to doubt what I have with William, I thought. He is a good person and a godly man who does the right thing and leads by example. In fact, I draw strength and encouragement from him. What I am saying is that when God puts his hand on you and causes things to happen, there is no room for doubt. I have grown tremendously in the Lord over the years and, spiritually, I am still growing each day. There is no need or reason to doubt Him, because He did say, "I will never leave or forsake you," As it turned out, the lady at church had dementia and it wasn't even Reverend Alford she was talking about. I never told him that my shoes were not the problem that day.

As the months faded away and I felt more and more attached to William, I also started to experience health problems again, but I drew strength from his presence. It seemed that physically, I had started to retrogress and every other day, I had a setback. I sometimes thought of but did not question why this was happening to me now. William was very understanding and concerned and always said, "We are going to pray that the Lord will guide the doctor's hand and let him fix your problem."

As time passed, I stopped working at the university, but kept up my volunteer and community work, thinking that would take my mind off me. William would call and come over, but we didn't go out a lot anymore. Occasionally, we will go places and I enjoyed those times, but I always had a headache and in the back of my mind I was thinking, this is not fair.

I finally got to the point where the medication was not working, and surgery was imminent. The tumor on the base of my brain was growing. I had surgery and afterward a period of convalescence. Believe me, it was a hard road back, but prayers and support made all the difference. After I went home from rehab, I was able to take care of myself, but I still had generalized onset seizures. When they occurred, I would be unconscious for just a little while, but afterward would not remember what happened just before. A decision had to be made. I was able to take care of myself, but the seizures were the problem. I discussed the situation with everybody because I wanted to do what was easier for them, thinking it was easier to go to one of them, than it was for one of them to uproot his/her life to come to me. They all said the same thing, we took care of you before and we will gladly do it again. Each of my children wanted me to come and live with them. My brother wanted me to come home to Georgia and live with him and his wife, arguing that there was plenty of space and the house was part mine anyway. Both of my younger sisters said they would do whatever was necessary. I would not hear of any of the offers because they had their own lives and I did not want to be in the way. William even stepped in and said, "Let's go ahead and get married and I can take care of you." I know that would have definitely been unfair. Finally, my sister living in New York moved n with me, because she was retired and could go to New York any ime she wanted to, if she needed to do that.

Months passed and the loving relationship that William and had was not going as well as it had gone in the past. I would go out to church and places with my sister, but I was just not as confident going with him or being around him for that matter. I didn't want him to see me have seizures. Sometimes, I would suggest to my sister that we go to New York to her house and stay three or four days, just to avoid him. He would call every day to check on both of us. He was patient. More than a year passed, and he was still patiently there for me.

One evening, William came over and insisted on me coming to his house for dinner. I said no at first because I had been out with my sister most of the day and felt a little tired. Then, I thought about it and reconsidered. We had a nice dinner and a long talk afterward. He started out by saying that we fell in love, as well as grew in love. He continued by telling me that he brought me over for two reasons that night. One reason was to show me that his house had whatever I needed and that he was capable of taking care of me. Then after a long pause he said that he had planned to ask me to marry him a long time ago, before I had surgery, but he waited. That, he said, was his first mistake. Then when he finally asked me after I got sick, he understood why I said no. He went on to say that I have no real reason to say no again and he was not going to make the same mistake again. Then he picked up the Bible that was lying on the counter and read I Corinthians, chapter 7 in its entirety. That chapter explains the idea of Christian liberty in the area of marital relations, morality, and the Christian concept of marriage; how Christians think about sex, marriage, and when they should or should not be married. When he finished, he said, "Now I need an answer. Will you marry me?"

I was not prepared for that question. I hesitated, then thought of all kinds of reasons why we should not get married now, starting with the reason that I didn't want to burden him. He let me finish then he asked, "Do you love me?" I slowly said yes. He put his arm around my shoulder and said that he loved me with all his heart, and he had been waiting to have me as his own for a long time. He went on to say that two people who are truly in love will work hard on the obstacles in the road and they will not run away from one another as soon as things get hard. When a man and woman really love one another, they will not allow anything to keep them apart.

I had always known that William loved me as much as I loved him, but I had never heard him express his love verbally, in such a way. Again, he asked me if I would marry him. I answered by asking him if he could give me some time. The fact of the matter was that I did not want to be a burden to him, and I was a little embarrassed about my seizures. He had never witnessed me having one and I didn't want him to. I tried to explain that the doctor said that in time, with my medical regiment, the seizures would go away completely, and I will be able to function as I always had. I could see that he was visibly upset. He shot back, "Didn't you just hear anything I said?"

GOLDEN NUGGETS FOR GROWTH #20

A piece of advice to those struggling in love or in any situation: Just remember that you have a direct channel to the Master. Just speak to Him, and He will hear you. More than that, He will hear you and give you what you need. The greatest opportunity that any believer has is to talk directly to God in prayer. He will accept your "pleases" "thank-yous" and "hallelujahs" but, most importantly, He will respond to your cry and give you what you need, if you will ask in faith.

The turning point in my life did not come until many years after my divorce and that was when I realized that what happened in my marriage to cause the breakup was beyond my control. However, I did have control of what happened after the fact. That turning point was when I sensed that someone was with me, a sensation that I had felt before. That sensation was reaching out to me and I recognized exactly what it was and what it was telling me...you have done the best that you knew how to do and now it is time to let it all go, so turn the corner and let the past go.

The more you talk to God, the more He will guide you to peace and harmony. At one time, I did not have that peace and harmony in my life but now because of the faith in and the love for God that I have, things have changed. I can ask him, and he will guide me to a right decision. Not only has he fixed many things that were broken in my life, but I firmly believed that he planted things at the right place, at the right time because He knew my needs.

WHAT SCRIPTURE SAYS ABOUT DEPENDING ON GOD TO REACH YOUR TURNING POINT:

Jeremiah 29:11 (ESV)--"For I know the plans I have for you, declares the Lord, plans for welfare and not for evil, to give you a future and a hope."

Philippians 4:19 (ESV)--"And my God will supply every need of yours according to his riches in glory in Christ Jesus."

John 6:63 (ESV)--"It is the Spirit who gives life; the flesh is no help at all. The words that I have spoken to you are spirit and life."

Exodus 14:14 (ESV)--"The Lord will fight for you, and you have only to be silent."

Jeremiah 33:3 (ESV)--"Call to me and I will answer you, and will tell you great and hidden things that you have not known."

John 15:4-5 (ESV)--"Abide in me, and I in you. As the branch cannot bear fruit by itself, unless it abides in the vine, neither can you, unless you abide in me. I am the vine; you are the branches. Whoever abides in me and I in him, he it is that bears much fruit, for apart from me you can do nothing."

Chapter 21: Moving with a Promise and a Prayer

Yes, William was visibly upset, something that I have never seen happen to him since I had known him. However, he didn't say a word and he didn't have to; his facial expression and body language said it all. He walked out of the room and when he came back his eyes were red, evidence that he had shed some tears. "Get your things and I'll take you home," he said. If a knife had been available, I could have cut the tension in the car with it. He said nothing the entire drive to my house. He got out and walked me to the door and said good night. As I unlocked the door, he stood there with his left hand in his pocket as he typically did. When the door was open, I turn to him and he just walked away, got in his car, and drove off.

When I went inside, my sister was in the den watching television. She called to me as I passed the door, "Why are you home so early? I really didn't expect you to be back until much later. Is everything OK?" she asked. I said yes, and then burst into tears. All I could say was "What have I done, what have I done?" I sat down on the bottom step to the second floor. She came out and sat down beside me. She knew that I always tried to stay away from people if I had any hint that I might have a seizure, so she asked if I had one while I was at William's house. Before I could answer she said, "If you did, it's alright, William loves you and he understands. Remember he stuck by you through the surgery and through your rehab and it's no big deal." I turned to her and buried my head in her shoulder and told her what had happened, every detail. She told me that she knew that we loved each other, and I needed to stop being afraid and stop thinking that I will be a burden to everybody. "We all love you and will do anything for you and you are not a burden, especially to that man and you need to tell him exactly how you feel," she continued. I told her that I knew she was right. Then I told her that I didn't want to discuss it anymore because I needed to go to bed and get some rest.

I went upstairs, took a hot bath and just soaked in the tub, talking to God, asking for guidance. I was so confused. I had faith in God, but I believed that I had lost hope in having someone love me and I was even questioning whether I even deserved to be loved again. After about an hour in the tub, I got out and went to bed, but I didn't go to sleep. I picked up the Bible from the nightstand and turned to I Corinthians chapter 7 and started to read. I had read the first nine verses when it hit me, and it was made as plain as day. William was struggling and trying to do the right thing. Now, what I knew I needed to do was walk completely out of his life and let him find himself a wife or become his wife.

I looked at the clock on the bedside table and it said 11:10. I really did not care what time it was. I picked up the phone and dialed the number. William answered on the second ring. When I said hello, he became alarmed, asking what was wrong. I replied, "Nothing is wrong, but everything is right. Yes, I will marry you." I think he threw the phone down and I waited, not knowing what to expect next. Then his voice came back on the phone, saying, "I know it's late but give me 20 minutes and then open the door."

I got up got dressed quickly and applied a little makeup. When the doorbell rang, my sister came out of her room putting on her robe. We met in the hall, she said, "Who can that be in the middle of the night and why are you dressed?" All I said was, "You will see." She followed me downstairs (probably thinking I had really lost my mind). She rushed ahead of me and peeped out the window and immediately opened the door. William brushed past her and grabbed me so tight that my feet left the floor. My sister turned around and said, "Well, I see what's going on. I will be upstairs."

He again got down on one knee, took a ring box out of his coat pocket, and asked me again if I would marry him. I said yes before he could finish the question. After we sat in the den awhile and talked about what changed my mind, I made some coffee and we talked some more. I told him that God laid it on my heart to reread I Corinthians chapter 7, because he had a message there for me and in that message was the decision that I needed to make. Then it dawned on me that he had on the very same thing he had on earlier that evening, even down to the tie. I asked him how he got dressed and back over here so fast. He told me that he had been driving around town after he dropped me off and then he went home and sat in his driveway for a long time debating if he should come back because he was dissatisfied with the way he left me. He said he had been in the house about five minutes when I called. Before we realized how long we had been talking, it was 2 o'clock in the morning, so he left and told me he would be back first thing in the morning.

As I locked the door and headed upstairs, I was trying to decide if I would wake up my sister and tell her the news now or wait until the morning. By the time I was at the top of the stairs, I had decided that I couldn't wait. I pushed her door open and walked in. She sat up in bed, saying come on in and share the news. She told me that she was not eavesdropping, but before she got to her room, she heard me tell him yes. "I held my breath, waiting for you to say the right answer before I came on in and went to bed," she said. We talked for a little while and then she suggested that I must be very tired and needed to get to bed. But to be truthful, I was no way tired that night.

William called the next morning about 8 o'clock while I was still sleeping. He asked my sister to call him when I was up and dressed. It was about 10 before I woke up and I remembered he said he was coming over. I jumped out of bed and ran to the bathroom as my sister stuck her head in the door and told me that he had called and would be over later. She also reminded me that I was supposed to meet one of the church members at lunch time to talk to her about a housing issue. She quickly said that she would call Sister Tate and ask her to take care of it for me. When she called Sister Tate, William had already shared the news with Reverend Tate, and she told my sister that I need not worry about my meeting with the member, she would handle everything.

William and I made some plans as we had breakfast-brunch. My sister and I contacted our family members together, to tell them the good news. To most of them it was not a surprise and they said they knew it would only be a matter of time. And, of course, you know the next call I made was to my best friend, Estheree. She told me she had been praying that it would happen since I got home from rehab. William does not have immediate family; he was an only child and his parents had been deceased for years. There were some cousins in Connecticut, but nobody close. We both wanted a wedding, but I felt shy about being before so many people right now for fear of a seizure. He understood and I had to put the brakes on my children and younger sisters because their wheels were already turning for a garden wedding at my house. We said thanks, but no thanks for right now.

We got married the next Friday at my church in Pastor Tate's office with my sister and one of my nieces who lived in Wilmington in attendance and, of course, Sister Tate. Since I was a child, I had always kept that nice outfit for special occasions. This I thought was a special occasion and I pulled out a royal-blue suit that I had been saving since last year when I purchased it. We promised that later, when I felt ready, we would have a larger wedding with a big reception. That Sunday morning, Reverend Alford preached a sermon like I had never heard him preach before. His subject was "A Prayer and a Promise." I sat there in the front pew and just took in every single word. On that Sunday after church, the members surprised us with a small reception in the fellowship hall. I should have known something was going on when I saw my children and all my other relatives who lived in the area in attendance at the morning service at his church.

Since I was a little girl, I had secretly wanted to be a preacher's wife. I would look at our pastor's wife back home and say she looks so pretty walking beside him in her fancy hats. That is probably one of the reasons I always wore a hat to church when I grew up. That first Sunday as Mrs. William Tyrell Alford, sitting there in my wide hat, I had to have been the proudest pastor's wife in the world. I say pastor's wife instead of first lady because everybody always gets it wrong when they say first lady. "First Lady" of the Church is not biblical and is a man-made title. The pastor's wife is not superior to anyone else in the church, so when that distinction is made for her it creates the appearance of partiality. It puts her above the other members and does not suggest a mutual respect that all believers are to give one another regardless of who they are. Distinguishing a pastor's wife by calling her "first lady" gives her an unnecessary level of prestige among the other women in the church. I asked the members not to refer to me as that because it sets a precedent of special privilege and entitlement that has no place in the church of God. Until this day they call me Sister Alford.

GOLDEN NUGGETS FOR GROWTH #21

Don't let your joy, peace and love die because of stubbornness. When you've done everything you think you know to do, then allow God to step in and do what you can't do. After you let him step in, trust him with all your heart and lean not to your limited understanding but submit to Him and He will help you move on. Just pray and He will do what He promises.

Do not be afraid to turn to God with your relationships. He will always be there for you and love you unconditionally no matter what decision you have made, because He can fix any mess you make. No matter what you, your partner, or your relationship may be facing, ask God to watch over you and guide your actions and your decisions.

As long as you live in this troubled world there will be issues. The evidence of faith is to follow God's lead and have the willingness to fight through those issues. If you trust God and believe that He will do it for you, you will come to a right decision.

Don't second guess yourself as I did in making a decision about marriage; just know that "God's got this" and believe that the only way you can really know what type of person you are committing to is to have faith in God and actually trust the person.

WHAT SCRIPTURE SAYS ABOUT UNCERTAINTY:

Matthew 6:34 (ESV)--"Therefore do not be anxious about tomorrow, for tomorrow will be anxious for itself. Sufficient for the day is its own trouble."

Psalm 62:8 (ESV)--"Trust in him at all times, O people; pour out your heart before him; God is a refuge for us."

Psalm 56:3 (ESV)--"When I am afraid, I put my trust in you."

2 Peter 3:9 (ESV)--"The Lord is not slow to fulfill his promise as some count slowness, but is patient toward you, not wishing that any should perish, but that all should reach repentance."

Philippians 4:6 (ESV)--"Do not be anxious about anything, but in everything by prayer and supplication with thanksgiving let your requests be made known to God."

Psalm 32:8 (ESV)--"I will instruct you and teach you in the way you should go; I will counsel you with my eye upon you."

Romans 8:28 (ESV)--"And we know that for those who love God all things work together for good, for those who are called according to his purpose."

Chapter 22: A Final Release

The week after we were married, both of us were busy getting things done. My new husband kept reminding me to take it easy and rest, but to me, I was busy, but it was not work. We chose to live in my house because it was larger and had four bedrooms and another room in the basement that could serve as a bedroom if we needed it to be, and a study, two living areas, and a sun porch. His house only had three bedrooms, not enough to have all my children and their families visit at the same time. He had a mover pack his things and move them to my house. There was a young couple in his congregation who had been married about six months and were not exactly where they wanted to be financially. They had been trying to get themselves together, so he rented his house to them with an option to buy, when they were able.

He said that he didn't really see any need to keep the house, although he bought it when he first went into the ministry because the only memories that he had in it were memories of him living by himself. William had been an only child. When he was in high school his father was killed in a car accident, leaving only him and his mother. The only other relative that he remembered was his grandmother's sister in Connecticut and an aunt in Arizona. He told me the story of how he got to Delaware in the first place. He received a scholarship to Delaware State and one to Liberty University in Virginia. He and his mother chose Delaware State.

Immediately after receiving his bachelor's degree, he got a vision to go into the ministry, so he enrolled at a famous Theological Seminary right here in Wilmington. He said that he drove home to Connecticut twice a month to see his mother. After he got his master's he enrolled in Divinity School in Durham, North Carolina. His mother joined him there for the two years he was a student. After receiving his doctorate, they came back to Wilmington and he got a teaching position at the seminary he graduated from and bought the house he presently owns. Before they could bring his mother's things from Connecticut and close her house there, she died. She was not sick, and an autopsy ruled that she died of natural causes. He said that it was almost as if she made sure he was equipped and alright before she went on to glory. He became pastor of Mt. Rainer Missionary Baptist Church and has been there since that time. What was so ironic was he was at the university in Durham the same year I got married the first time and moved to Durham when I worked at Research Triangle Park.

My sister moved back to her house in New York and as the months passed, I got better and better. The seizures came less and less frequently. After some time, they stopped altogether, and I was back to my old self again. By then, winter was almost over, and my family brought up the wedding again. Over my protest, William took their side and ganged up on me. Because it was not quite warm enough yet, we had the "real" wedding at my house.

The house was decorated so beautifully. All my family came and some of my friends from around Wilmington as well as some of his closest friends. Elizabeth came up from home and, of course, Estheree and her husband came from Texas. My children wanted to invite Carl's sister, Darlene, and she came. Carl did not come but he sent his well wishes and tucked away in his gift was a card saying, "I never thought you would throw in the towel before me."

Reverend Tate preformed the ceremony on a crisp winter Saturday in 2017, and this time Estheree was the matron of honor and several of my friends were bridesmaids, along with several of William's friends in the ministry as groomsmen. Elizabeth took over the music and she and Sister Tate presented a beautiful program of wedding music with the organist from our church as musician. I chose a beige below-the-knee-length dress with short train attached and a beige pill box hat. As I stood at the top of the stairs, looking down in the foyer at my handsome son waiting to escort me into the sun room, I thought I must have been dreaming, because I was almost positive that I saw Carl step out of my son and wave goodbye as he left through the dining room. I said to myself, I am not dreaming and I took a breath and thought, thank you, God, for letting him release.

The reception was held at the Ministers' Club downtown. It was like a fairy tale. William and I skipped the first dance and instead made a marriage declaration to each other. As I finished my speech, I felt a lightness as if the old me had walked out of my life and a new me was there. That, I thought, was my final release.

We didn't go to the Bahamas, but we did take a four-day "real" honeymoon to Niagara Falls, New York. When we returned, I decided that doing volunteer work was not enough. So, I went back to work at the university in the research department on a part-time basis.

GOLDEN NUGGETS FOR GROWTH #22

It can be frustrating when you continually caution yourself about what happened in the past, repeatedly. Too many of us are so busy living in the past that we cannot fully get comfortable with living in the present. We are going to have issues from our past, but at some point, we must deal with them before we can proceed on with our lives, the plan that God has for us. Some of us are so wrapped up with things that happened in our past that we literally cannot get beyond being stuck in a rut and living a normal productive life in the now. Before we can move forward, we have to first learn how to let our past just be our past and grow from the experience.

A past relationship can be one of the biggest teachers in helping us learn how to heal from a misfortune, and sometimes it's not a misfortune but something from which you just can't move on. It's all about figuring out why you keep going back. When you're able to release the past and let go of things whether they are weighing you down or just keeping you looking back, you can move forward and have the life you really want. Simply say, "I am not my own, because I belong to Jesus and I know He knows what's best for me." Then trust Him and He will help you release the past. As you think about making plans and decisions, pray about it. Through prayer and spiritual growth, we can more easily put our past behind us and move forward. I did and I now know that every storm has an expiration date.

WHAT SCRIPTURE SAYS ABOUT LEAVING THE PAST BEHIND:

Philippians 3:13 (NIV)--"Brothers and sisters, I do not consider myself yet to have taken hold of it. But one thing I do: Forgetting what is behind and straining toward what is ahead."

Isaiah 43:18 (NIV)--"Forget the former things; do not dwell on the past."

Ephesians 4:22-23 (ESV)--"Put off your old self, which belongs to your former manner of life and is corrupt through deceitful desires, and to be renewed in the spirit of your minds."

Chapter 23: The Right Relationship Comes at a Price

William and I had a wonderful life as husband and wife, but our happiness came at a price. He was busy in the ministry and teaching part time at the seminary and I was helping with several ministries in the church and volunteering in the community, as well as working part time at the university. We still had plenty of time together because, essentially, we were together mostly, especially when we were doing ministry projects. William started calling me "his beautiful wig lady." When I had treatments after my pancreatic cancer, my hair fell out, but it came back thick and bushy. However, when my head was shaved to have the tumor removed, it only came back in patches and it was very thin, forcing me to wear a wig. I had about a half dozen made, but I had one special favorite that I wore when I wasn't wearing a hat. It looked exactly like my hair used to look. All in all, I had gotten used to wearing them. I always wore a scarf or something on my head when I was at home. At night when I got ready for bed, I removed everything. He liked to run his fingers through the stringy locks I had left and call me curly locks. He often said, "I wouldn't trade these few locks for all the hair in the world."

The day that I went for my annual checkup, my life was again changed, in a very powerful way. It was an ordinary day and I felt good. I had, however, experienced occasional back pain, but in my opinion, nothing to worry about. I had my check up and the nurse was on the phone making the appointment for an MRI just to look at the scar tissue from the brain surgery. I jokingly said, "You probably should be ordering a scan of my back also, because it has been giving me problems lately." As soon as she got off the phone, she asked me more about the back pain and then told me to wait before I left the office. When she returned, she told me the doctor wanted to talk to me again. He asked me about the symptoms and the intensity of the pain in my back. Then he said, "Given your history, I guess we need to get a CT scan of your stomach and back also, but it's nothing for you to be worried about." Two days later William drove me to the hospital to get my tests done. When we finished, we had a late lunch and decided to go home and relax for the remainder of the day. On the way home, he asked if I was feeling OK, saying that I looked pale. I told him that I was fine, just had a little back ache. The next day, I got a call from the doctor's office. The doctor wanted to see me that afternoon. William was teaching a class that day, so I drove myself. I wasn't even worried because it had not even dawned on me that anything was out of the ordinary.

When I arrived, I had to wait for about 10 minutes, so I made a nail appointment while I waited, hoping I wouldn't be at the doctor's office too long. As the nurse ushered me into his office and not an exam room, I still was not worried because I was thinking that he just wanted to share the results of my tests. I took a seat across from where he was sitting and he immediately got up, walked around his desk, and sat in a chair beside me. I can remember every word he said just as it was yesterday. He said, "Mrs. Alford, I know you are a fighter because I have been down that war road with you, and we are going to equip ourselves for battle again. I have some news and some more news." I gripped the arm of the chair and said, "OK, what is it?" He told me that my MRI showed there was something there, but he would need additional test to determine the seriousness of it. However, there was no questions about the CT scan results, there was a growth about two inches from my spine and he suspected that was the culprit that was causing the discomfort in my back. Everything after that statement was a blur. He went on to say that he was glad that I shared about the backache and that something had to be done right away. I felt myself fly up out of the chair saying no, no absolutely not, no more surgery! He called the nurse in and asked her to bring in, I don't remember what, to calm me down and then called my husband.

I was out of control. I told them they could not call my husband or anybody else. I sat back down and told him I didn't need anything to calm me down. We talked some more, and he said that it was not wise for me to put off the surgery. He also told me that this is something that I should not try to go through by myself. Not taking no for an answer, he said he would have his nurse make an appointment for tomorrow when I was calm to discuss more about the procedure. I sat in the courtyard outside his office until I got myself together. Then I called the one person, other than my husband, that I could share anything with: Estheree. She has always been my friend. As Shannon Adler says, "A best friend is the only one that walks into your life when the world has walked out." That was Estheree.

When Estheree picked up the phone, I had doubts about even telling her. The words would not come out of my mouth, so instead I asked her what she was doing. "Polishing silverware," she said, "but I know you didn't call me to ask what I am doing. What's wrong and don't tell me nothing because I can hear it in your voice," she said. I told her the whole story and said I didn't know what to do, so I did the next best thing and called her. She said, "Well, the first thing you are going to do is hang up that phone and call William so he can come pick you up. Then you are going to tell him and together, you will decide when you will have the surgery. By the time you make the decision, I will be there." I let her finish giving me orders then I said, "First of all, I am not having surgery and second of all, I am not going to tell anybody, and I don't want you to either." She shot back, "Bev, I don't want to sound insensitive at a time like this but I have to say this, I will honor your wishes not to tell your children and siblings because you need to do that yourself, but if you don't tell William, I will. Now hang up and do what I said. I will call him in 30 minutes to see if you are with him." With that, she hung up the phone.

Deep down inside, I knew she was right because William and I never kept secrets and I could not get through this without his support. Besides, if something went wrong and I had not told him, I would have a high price to pay. So, I called William. He had just dismissed his class and walked to his office when I called. As soon as he said hello, I burst into tears and he could not understand what I was saying. I did manage to tell him I was at Central Plaza at the doctor's office and I needed him to come get me. He was there almost immediately. I could not tell the story again, so he went to the nurse after I stopped crying. The doctor came out and told him that he needed to see us in his office the next morning at 9 o'clock. William left my keys with the receptionist and called one of the church members to arrange to get my car from the parking garage.

When we got home, he must have held me for an hour before I was able to tell him the news. I just sat there and rocked back and forth saying, "I am so sorry." He sat down on the floor in front of me and told me I had nothing to be sorry about. He reminded me that I was his wife and he promised to take care of me and stay with me as long as he lived. Then he reminded me that nothing is too big for God and we will go to the doctor's office tomorrow and find out what the prognosis is and proceed from there. I went to bed and he fixed me hot tea and soup. I must have drifted off to sleep because when I woke up it was dark outside and he was sitting beside the bed with the laptop in his lap. He looked over and said, "Oh, you are finally awake. I have been trying to do a little research about this, so I won't be ignorant when we visit the doctor tomorrow," he said. We talked more about it and asked him not to tell the children just yet, suggesting that we wait until we had some promising news to tell them. I did agree however, that I would do whatever the doctor suggested.

The next morning, we went back to see the doctor and he told us that the growth in my back had to come out immediately and treatment after that would depend on it being benign or malignant. He added that he suspected it was an extension of the first cancer. My doctor was one of the best in the state and he wanted to set the surgery at one of the best hospitals on the East Coast in Baltimore in two days. I was a wreck physically, emotionally, and mentally and William and my doctor knew it. had done research on the holistic approach they use at Cancer Treatment Centers and I told my doctor and William that I wanted to visit one of the centers before I underwent any surgery. My doctor did not like the idea of waiting, but he went along with it. did not want to tell my children yet, and I persuaded William to just indulge me at least until we could see if the Cancer Center could help me with my emotional as well as my physical state.

I called my son and told him that we were going out of town for a couple of weeks and would see them when we got back. I called him because he didn't ask a lot of questions like my daughters and my sisters. The only thing my son said was, "Boy, the two of you are forever going to some conference or convention." I did not confirm or deny it; I just laughed. There is a Cancer Center in Philadelphia, but we felt it was too close to where we lived to keep it a secret. So, my doctor made a referral at the center near my home in Georgia, a short drive from Atlanta's Hartsfield-Jackson International Airport. We left the next day. When we got to the Cancer Center, my condition was confirmed.

I felt a little better about being there having experienced cancer experts who are committed to delivering comprehensive, integrative care. The doctors and clinicians collaborated, shared knowledge, and coordinated treatments to provide multidisciplinary care tailored to my needs. I was there three days before the surgery was scheduled. The night before surgery I was very nervous, and they all came in and talked me through every step. Later that night, I told William that things had happened so fast that I had not even had a chance to think about why all of this was happening to me or what would happen if the surgery did not go well. "What if I can't walk after the surgery?" I asked. He got into the hospital bed beside me and said, "And if you can't walk when this is over, I will still take care of you. God has promised us

His strength. He will never give you a trial you cannot handle and you can call on His power at any time, for he said in Isaiah 41:10 (NIV) "Do not fear, for I am with you; do not be dismayed, for I am your God. I will strengthen you and help you; I will uphold you with my righteous right hand." He also told me that God put us together so he could comfort and take care of me and God would do the rest.

I had surgery the next day and it went well. After another 10 days of holistic treatment and therapy, we went home. We called the family together and told them what had happened. They were upset that we didn't see fit to share with them, but they were thankful that it was over. The surgery was a complete success and after maintenance treatments thing should be fine. Of course, I had to tell them about the spot on my brain that had redeveloped, and we still had to deal with that. After a lot of back and forth and decisions, which I had the last say about, I chose drug theory to retard the growth of the brain tumor. I knew I was taking a real chance and it was a high price to pay, but I also knew that God was the most experienced doctor.

GOLDEN NUGGETS FOR GROWTH #23

Do we always confront life's toughest choices with sound logic, or do we let our emotions make choices for us? Usually, our emotions factor in far too often when we are making important decisions. We know that man is horrible in terms of relying on emotions to make decisions, and yet almost all our decisions are based on the emotions we feel about a situation. That is why we should include loved ones in major decision making, especially if it is a decision that will affect them, too. We do have a right to be selfish, but in situations where other people will be affected, it is fair that we should include them or at least give them the opportunity to know why we made a choice.

Major decisions can have lasting effects as well as completely change lives; therefore, consideration should be given to all parties involved as well as the opportunity for them to weigh in even if they don't actually help make the decision. Relationships are critical in our lives and they can be destroyed when big decisions are made that affect others without considering what they think. Making such decisions can also be unhealthy.

If we look closely, we can see that God supplies us with some instructions on how we should serve, not only the Lord, but serve others and let them serve us as well. Sometimes, it takes personal situations to recognize that a lesson, even if it is one that has been learned before, is worth taking into consideration. Because God said, "Lean not to your own understanding." Sometimes, we lean but forget to listen and understand. When you have a problem to solve, especially if it will alter your loved ones' life, it is far better if you allow them to be there for you. To do anything less is being selfish.

WHAT SCRIPTURE SAYS ABOUT BEING SELFISH:

Philippians 2:4 (ESV)--"Let each of you look not only to his own interests, but also to the interests of others."

Galatians 6:2 (ESV)--"Bear one another's burdens, and so fulfill the law of Christ."

Philippians 2:3 (ESV)--"Do nothing from rivalry or conceit, but in humility count others more significant than yourselves."

Chapter 24: Looking Back and Understanding

William and I were married about a year when my health problems took a downhill turn again. But thank God, he was a man of strength and a man of God. My husband showed me love, he shielded and protected me as we walked together, down that path to recovery. I am not there yet, but I no longer feel guilty about having him help take care of me. Now, as I get ready for the summer of 2019, there has been tremendous improvement in my condition but I still have concerns. However, I am not in this alone. I have a loving husband and family to support me and a God that will never leave me alone, so I am covered. My life goes on as normal as I can make it. I still do many of the things that I enjoy doing; I even went back to work at the university for a time. After a while, my body told me that it was a bit much to continue that. Occasionally, I have to take to the bed, but for the most part, I am active and can do most of the things I always did.

Through all of this I have come to realize that I am truly blessed. With that said, I make a promise...I will never speak of ill health ever again because Jesus said, "For my yoke is easy to bear, and the burden I give you is light." Sooo, I am determined to receive and bear that burden.

Yes, life is good, I am enjoying family and friends and I get to travel and do a lot of things with my husband, grandchildren, and whomever I choose. But I mostly enjoy sitting in the front pew at Mt. Rainer Missionary Baptist Church on Sunday mornings, styling one of my favorite hats, listening to God through the person of the Rev. Dr. William Tyrell Alford, my husband.

I want to live in the comfort and Grace of God. I want Him to be a part of every decision and action I make because now I see and understand. When I was a child, I did not realize how blessed I truly was. I followed the lead of something inside me that I could not identify but knew was tugging at my heart to act. As I grew older, I realized how blessed I have been all those years, because that something IS the Comforter. That Comforter that I encountered when I was 2 years old has stayed with me through trials and tribulations, sickness and death, love, marriage, divorce and true love again. That Comforter has been with me through valley disappointments and mountaintop experiences, as I helped others and as I was helped by others—and all that time before I ever knew it, that Comforter was THE COMFORTER, who has never left or forsaken me through these 69 years. YES, IT IS A GOOD DAY!

Afterword

I hope the reader will draw strength from situations on these pages about life as seen through the main character, Beverly Martin; where she has been and where God brought her from. I also hope that the reader will realize that God never fails us; all we must do is believe and wait on Him. I also hope that the reader will understand that you should not be bitter about things in your past, just get better at living in the now because there is a big difference between bitter and better, and the difference is the letter "I." I had to make the choice. Each of us gets to make the choice.

This fiction story is about an all-powerful presence that is always looking out for our interests. This presence is much more powerful than a family member or a best friend who never leaves. Beverly followed this presence; this voice inside her heart calling on her to act throughout her early life. However, in adulthood her moral compass and love collided with that voice, putting her on a collision course with life. She passed up opportunities of which she could have taken advantage. Instead, she walked away from life's demands, away from acceptance, love, companionship, and happiness as it weighed over her like a shadow. However, later in life, she came to an awakening and realized that God never said everything would be easy or that any of us will get everything that makes us happy. There is no place in the Bible that says we shall be happy all the time...but it does say that we can have joy and peace.

Although she knew she was not afraid of dying, she found her truth: that she was actually afraid of living. In the end she realized that security does not rest in our circumstances, instead it rests in being loved by God. She learned that if she kept her hand in His hand, she need not be afraid of living or dying. With that she was able to release and move on with her life.

"Therefore, as we have opportunity, let us do good to all people, especially to those who belong to the family of believers" Galatians 6:10 (NIV).

About the Author

Shirley A. Johnson grew up in rural Enfield, North Carolina, and she enjoys the simplicity of rural living and good friends, but most of all she values her relationship with God. She has been divorced for 37 years and has three grown children and three precious grandchildren. She believes that God carefully calibrates the amount of difficulty one will encounter each day and He knows exactly how much one can handle, with His help.

She also believes that God's love is ever lasting, and she refers often to I John 4:18, (KJV): "There is no fear in love; but perfect love casteth out fear: because fear hath torment. He that feareth is not made perfect in love."

When we experience God's love in our lives and share it with others, we do not need to fear. The two-way relationship of God's love in our lives gives us confidence and security. Most importantly, she knows that God teaches us to love everybody, even those who hurt us along the way.

God has a way of reaching into the darkest of places and shining a light that you never knew was there. In this fictionalized story, Beverly Martin learns to get through the trials and tribulations of life, from fearing a hobo and a sister's teasing to surviving the school years and discrimination and first love, marital infidelity and divorce, and then life-threatening illnesses. She draws strength from God and never fails to believe and wait on Him. Beverly is nourished by this divine guidance because there is a difference between bitter and better, and the difference is the letter "I." Each of us gets to make that choice.

CPSIA information can be obtained
at www.ICGtesting.com
Printed in the USA
FSHW022001221220
76895FS

9 781736 122709